DOWN
BOOK II OF THE
NO BOUNDARIES SERIES

Karen Cavalli

Lavender Press
An imprint of Blue Fortune Enterprises LLC

DOWN
Copyright © 2021 by Karen Cavalli.

All rights reserved. Printed in the United States of America. No part of this book may be used or reproduced in any manner whatsoever without written permission except in the case of brief quotations embodied in critical articles or reviews.

This book is a work of fiction. Names, characters, businesses, organizations, places, events and incidents either are the product of the author's imagination or are used fictitiously. Any resemblance to actual persons, living or dead, events, or locales is entirely coincidental.

For information contact :
Blue Fortune Enterprises, LLC
Lavender Press
P.O. Box 554
Yorktown, VA 23690
http://blue-fortune.com

Book and Cover design by Wesley Miller, WAMCreate

ISBN: 978-1-948979-54-2
First Edition: February 2021

DEDICATION

To the Virginia Beach Friends Meeting in Virginia Beach, Virginia, the first place I experienced sacred silence in the company of others.

To the Sisters and staff of St. Paul's Monastery in St. Paul, Minnesota, who welcomed me without question and provided sacred space and time for silent retreats when funds were scarce at an earlier time in my life. Through and because of the Sisters, who live a monastic life in the Benedictine tradition, my understanding and experience of silence blossomed. During one of my retreats at the St. Paul Monastery I felt the palpable net of protection the Sisters' prayers wove around the Monastery and knew, at least in my perception, how the invisible could become varying degrees of concrete.

To Kay Deblock (her last name when I knew her) who when I was a teen impressed me with her kindness and understanding. Those qualities bridged the gap in my understanding when it came to her faith life; at that age, I just didn't get it, but if Kay was fervent about it? Well, there must be something to it. That bridge provided an opening when I encountered the St. Paul Monastery and allowed me to let go of concerns I did not share the same belief system; the gifts were there for all.

Praise for other titles by Karen Cavalli:

Bad Mind

Karen Cavalli writes movingly and well about her life, which has been enriched throughout by otherworldly experiences. She describes her interactions with the people, in the flesh and in the spirit, who have touched her life and who have been touched, in turn, by hers. Some of her experiences are "encounters with aliens." All of her life has been filled with emotionally and spiritually rich events that illuminate the strength and survival of her own spirit as well as the strength of the human spirit.
Don C. Donderi, PhD
Associate Professor (retired)
McGill University, Montreal

Wildly cool. Both academic and curious. This woman knows a lot, and she's good at expressing it in an interesting fashion-she never makes you feel less than, or uninformed. Her work is a discovery that leads you to a milky revelation: there's so much you've missed already. Bad Mind invites you to resee the world you live in. Bravo.
Tom Chiarella

Undercover Goddess

I am very excited that this book is going to be part of a trilogy! I found *Undercover Goddess* to be mythical, fantastical, and incredibly interesting! This is another very unique book with incredible world-building that is very well done! I love the matriarchal/Amazonian feel of the narrative and the cover is stunning! There are so many facets and interesting story lines in this book!
The plot and pacing were good! I'm excited for the next books in this series! I also enjoyed the character development of Mave. The variety and composition of the characters was so unique! It is really a great book! I will be looking forward to more novels from

this author!
Katie P., Bookbustle

A quick read that whispers secrets from the time before the patriarchy
Cavalli weaves mysticism and fantasy in this powerful saga of strong women entwined in the changing threads of history. Women's roles are forever changed as new gods claim allegiance in an alien, yet sadly familiar, world. Mave bows to her destiny with the Ssha lizard people who speak in mind-verse and with the sexually amorphous half-and-half she loves. I loved seeing the sweeping cultural changes from Mave's perspective and experiencing her transformation from innocence to wisdom. I found Mave's relationship with the horses heart-warming. Fresh world-building, fast-paced action.
Teresa, Amazon Review

A superb Fantasy!
This novel is unlike anything I have read recently. I think that it is a great testament to the imagination of a writer that I can say that. There is a lot going on and a lot to understand since you are diving into a new world. Cavalli navigates that effortlessly and keeps us wanting more through the entire book, while ultimately leaving us satisfied, yet needing the next book!
R.K. Emery, Goodreads Review

Table of Contents

Prologue:	First Landing	8
Chapter 1:	Beatt	22
Chapter 2:	A Girl Who Can't Say No	26
Chapter 3:	Beatt Seeks Guidance at Apollonoulous	45
Chapter 4:	A Disturbance Between Venus and Earth	55
Chapter 5:	Beatt Hides Then is Seen	58
Chapter 6:	Descent	64
Chapter 7:	Heart of Beatt	72
Chapter 8:	Oblation Station	76
Chapter 9:	The Uses of Frost	91
Chapter 10:	Manifestation	101
Chapter 11:	It Begins	110
Chapter 12:	A Blow to the Soul	112
Chapter 13:	Home is Oblation	128
Chapter 14:	The Gateway Opens	134
Chapter 15:	The Invisible Goes to Work	145
Chapter 16:	The Redemption of the Dark	162
Preview of Book Three, Chapter One		179
About the Author		191

Prologue
First Landing

DACE BANKS, EIGHT YEARS OLD, raised Barbie's arm to wave goodbye to Mom, who stood at the door slipping on her sandals. Dad perched on the edge of the couch, feet planted apart in ready position, and studied *The Virginian Pilot* lying open on the ottoman as though studying a manual. He had a short leave from his job flying jets for the Navy in nearby Norfolk and had taken them on a long-promised vacation to Virginia Beach's First Landing State Park.

Mom straightened and flipped the ends of her long, sandy hair over her shoulders. She tugged on both ends of the self-tie of her denim wrap skirt, like a parachutist checking that her harness straps were secure. "I think they're coming," she said. "The feeling is so strong, just like before, the day they came to get me when I was a teenager living here."

Dad raised his head. "You mean before you started dating me and you never had another one of those nightmares?"

"Yes, my sweet," she said, swooping in to kiss him. "It's true, my other-worldly friends stopped coming to call once you were in the picture. Maybe they've had you on probation since then, and now that you've passed, they feel it's safe to come back. The feeling is centered on the beachfront of the park. I think I should go down there."

Dad frowned.

"Can I come?" Dace asked.

"Dace," started Dad.

"Of course she can, Connor!" Mom said. "It's just a walk on the beach."

He stood. "I want you back in half an hour."

"An hour," countered Mom. She sidled close to him and brushed the backs of her fingers on his cheek.

His upright posture softened, as Dace had observed it always did when Mom drew close.

"All right," said Dad. "No, wait, I take that back; fifty minutes."

"Fine." Mom smiled. She chucked him under the chin as he saw them to the door. "Not afraid of aliens, are you?"

"Can't be afraid of what doesn't exist," he said and kissed her cheek. "I'm only concerned about what does exist." He handed Dace his compass and a pocket atlas with maps of Virginia. "This will be good practice for you, Dace." He'd recently taught her how to navigate using a compass, the stars, and the invisible lines that crisscrossed the earth. "Latitude and longitude," he'd said, and when Dace's forehead creased in confusion, he amended, "Or just lat and long." He pronounced the g in long like the g in orange, just like her French teacher said the g in the word longue, which also meant long.

Dace pocketed the items and held Barbie by the torso as she followed Mom out the door. She turned to look back at Dad who glanced at his watch then turned to go back inside the house.

They walked down the path from their cabin to the boardwalk that led them out of the woods and onto the beach. The sun was just setting behind the gray clouds.

At the shoreline of First Landing, Mom and Dace stood facing the waves, their toes just out of reach of the of the ebbing tide.

Dace stood silently as Mom closed her eyes and lifted her heart to the ocean. After a moment, she sighed and opened her eyes. "Nothing." She shook her head. "I don't understand. The signal was so strong."

The sun inched down below the gun-metal waves. The lights of the hotels and homes that bookended the park's beach popped on like fireflies.

Mom rubbed her left brow, blinked, and turned her head back and forth. "I'm getting the pixels of light," she said.

Dace looked questioningly at her.

"An ophthalmic migraine," she explained. She covered her left eye with one hand. "Shoot. One's definitely coming on. I'm getting the fractured light in my side vision. Haven't had one of these for a long time. I used to get them after the visitors appeared to me. But why would one come before a visit?"

"Does it hurt, Mom?" Dace asked.

Mom shook her head. "There's no pain, just temporary blindness." Dace's eyes widened.

"Oh, not to worry. The eye doctor said years ago they happen to some people. He said avoid bright lights if one comes on and get to darkness." Mom cocked her head, and to Dace it seemed her gaze went out of focus, as though she truly were not seeing anything. "If I relax and don't look too hard, it's actually kind of cool. This crazy, multi-colored slinky-like worm circles more and more tightly and takes over my vision."

DOWN

Worry churned in the pit of Dace's stomach. "Mom!" Dace said, tugging on her hand. "Shouldn't we get to darkness?"

"Just a few more minutes." Mom held her hand over one eye, then the other.

The lights along the boardwalk came on in the deepening dusk.

"Oh dear," Mom said, "the pixelated slinky worm is taking over. We'd better find some darkness." She turned and blinked at the sand and the woods beyond. "We'll head for Bald Cypress Trail, which I'm pretty sure is past the dunes and to the left."

Taking Dace's hand, Mom stumbled up the dunes then veered left as the sand gave way to a grassy path.

"Can you see the opening to the trail?" Mom asked Dace, squinting at the woods.

"Yes, over there." Dace pointed to a spot a few feet away. She pulled her mother along the few feet of the path and into the dark, marshy woods of Bald Cypress Trail.

Under the marsh's tree canopy, Mom stopped and faced Dace. She blindly patted Dace's arms then her shoulders.

"Are you okay?" She cupped Dace's face. Behind them, the ocean shushed along the shoreline.

Dace placed her hands over her mother's, pressing their warmth into her cheeks, as her eyes adjusted to the gloom.

Dace paused, considering what Dad would say. "I'm fine," she said.

And she was for a moment, not really minding the dark, but then the feathers, or so it seemed, brushed the fine hairs at her nape and announced the awakening of slumbering creatures. The gossamer fringe rose then she sensed the presences. Here in the woods she felt the heartbeats of the nocturnal creatures waking up to the dark.

The golden eyes of a critter low to the ground winked at

Dace from the bushes. Another pair joined them, then a third.

Dace's heart raced. She patted the pocket with Dad's compass and atlas. Still there. She secured Barbie by the ankles. "Mom, I know what to do," Dace said.

"What, honey?" Mom asked.

Dace slid Barbie's head under Mom's palm. Her mother wrapped her hand around Barbie's plastic head with its bouffant of black hair and held it, considering.

"How would Barbie get us home?" Mom asked. "Maybe we should just stay here in the cypress grove until the migraine passes."

The golden eyes winked out all at once. Something rustled on the other side of the trail, only a few feet from them.

"Not Barbie, Mom, the star. The star can get us home," Dace said. "Dad taught me how on our first night here, when he taught me about directions and latta—" She paused. "Lat and long," she finished.

She turned and pointed to the sky beyond them framed by the entrance to the trail. Her mother looked without seeing. Dace dropped her arm. "If we can get back to the beach, I can find Polaris. Where we're staying is south of the beach. Dad told me. We just need to find Polaris, turn in the opposite direction, go down the boardwalk and after three cabins go right, and we'll be at our cabin. Here," Dace said, again taking Mom's hand and curling her fingers around Barbie's head. "You hold Barbie's head, and I'll hold her feet. I'll lead us home. Just follow my footsteps."

Her mother's forehead wrinkled in confusion. "Isn't Polaris a star? And don't the stars move in the night sky?"

Dace nodded. "Yes, but Dad said that Polaris doesn't move because that's the star that is always in the North."

Her mother sighed. "Right, the North Star. I was so certain

we were supposed to be out here tonight. But so be it. It wasn't meant to be." She grasped Barbie's head. "Ready."

Dace turned back to face the path leading out of the woods. She kept a light hold on Barbie's feet resting on her shoulder as she stepped carefully along the well-groomed path, her mother's cautious footsteps behind her.

When Dace cleared the woods, she paused to find the Big Dipper constellation then followed its southern edge up to the tip of the handle of the Little Dipper—the North Star. At the sight of it something deep inside Dace relaxed.

"How're we doing there, cap'n?" Mom asked.

"I found Polaris," she said. "I can get us home."

"Lead on," Mom said. "I sure can't. What a crazy light show I've got going on behind my lids."

Dace kept her eye on Polaris as she trudged through the dunes with her mother close behind. Dace envisioned the invisible lines that crisscrossed the earth, lines her dad and satellites used to navigate. Lat and long, lat and long, she repeated silently to herself.

"I'm a little sad," Mom said. "I thought sure something was going to happen tonight. I wouldn't have brought you out here if my intuition hadn't been so strong. Still is. Now your dad's got another reason to not believe in these things, and you'll be on his side, two against one."

Dace slogged up a dune. Grains of sand ground like tiny diamonds into the skin under the straps of her Jelly sandals. Dace liked that her mom aligned her with her dad. They could be a team. "Mom, no," Dace said, "It's better than that. It's two to watch out for you."

They climbed up the crest of the dune.

"Wait, Dace," Mom said, coming to a halt. "I'm sensing something." Her voice dropped to a whisper. "I knew we were supposed to be here tonight."

Dace turned to face Mom who nosed the air, her eyes still closed.

"Mom, come on, no," Dace said. Her legs trembled and her stomach hurt. "There's nothing here. Let's just go home."

What would Dad do? Dace stared out at the dark shoreline beyond her mother. A twinkle in the spindrift caught her eye. Instead of falling back with the spray, it grew into a glittering shape. Dace stood very still. The shape, not far from where she and her mother had stood, took on the figure of a person. As the shape solidified, the outline suggested the broad-shoulders and slim hips of a creature about as tall as her father. The shimmering shape swung back and forth at the waist, as though enjoying a new physical freedom. A long tail of hair bound at the back of the neck swung as well. Then the shape came to stillness. The hollows of his eye sockets glowed with diffuse light. He directed his gaze at Dace and Mom. Alarm sounded in the pit of Dace's stomach then spread to her legs and arms.

"Dace," Mom whispered. "What is it?"

Lat, long, lat, long, Dace said frantically to herself, then the feeling that her head might blow apart calmed.

The waves continued their noisy crash on the beach. The foam from the breaking waves eddied up and back. The spindrift was again just saltwater spray.

"Nothing," Dace told Mom. "I didn't see anything. Just the moon on the surf. Hold on to Barbie's head, Mom, I've got to get us home." Dace turned back to resume leading them out of the dunes and beach grass.

Once they reached the boardwalk, the warm lights of the cabins glowed through the trees. Their cabin was three beyond these first two, off a little jog in the boardwalk. Dace looked over her shoulder to double-check Polaris was still at her back.

"Honey," Mom said, "Wait for a minute." She released her hold on Barbie's head.

Dace turned, dangling Barbie by the feet. She glanced quickly at the surf; no half-man, half-sea being with glowing eyes. *Go, go,* her inner wingman ordered.

A beaming smile broke over Mom's face. "I can see!" she said. "The blindness cleared up just after I had that sense something was there."

"Nothing was there," Dace said. "I looked." Dace refused to believe a man-creature was out there. That's what Dad would do. He would probably even say she must have been influenced by her mother's insistence on the visitors.

Mom stepped alongside Dace and placed her arm around her shoulders. "I guess I'll never get you or your dad to believe in what I sense," she said.

Dace edged away from Mom and faced Polaris with arms extended fully out.

"What are you doing?" Mom asked.

"What Dad taught me. My nose knows Polaris is north. Opposite is south, and my writing hand is east."

"What about west?" Mom asked, grinning.

Dace shook her head. "Dad hasn't taught me west yet."

"You're such a good little worker," Mom said, hugging her. "I think you and I have had enough lessons for one night. Let's go home."

Dace felt proud and grounded. I'm a good worker, she thought, as she reached for her Mom's hand and guided them along the boardwalk, counting cabins.

She halted. "Mom," she said, turning to look up, "you said home."

Mom laughed. "I'm sure I meant our vacation rental. It's not home, I know, not really, not yet." She clapped her hand over her mouth.

"Mom!" Dace said. "What? Do we have to leave Norfolk?"

"I wasn't supposed to tell yet," her mother said. "Your dad and a Navy buddy who's getting out soon too want to start a company to... hm, I'm not sure exactly how to say it, but basically figure out a way to develop and sell the system the Navy uses with satellites. It's how your dad and the other pilots navigate."

"Lat and long, I know," said Dace.

"Yes, the system uses lat and long but the satellites allow them to make it easier to use. Dad says they could put it in cars, and the satellites would use lat and long to tell the car which way to go. No more maps!"

Dace patted her pocket with the compass and miniature atlas. "If there were no more maps, what would I carry instead?"

"I don't know. But your dad says the military has okayed non-military people to develop it and sell to civilians. That's what your dad and his buddy are going to do."

A soft wing stroked Dace's nape. Two glinting circles bobbed up the beach toward them.

"Okay, let's go."

Mom laughed and trotted after Dace as she ran along the boardwalk and turned right at the third cabin. Dad's energy radiated toward her like a beacon. She could never tell Mom or Dad that she felt things like this. Her mother would be overjoyed she was following in her footsteps and set out to home-school her in her magical beliefs, and she would lose her newly defined, special connection with Dad: protecting her mother.

"Come on, Mom," Dace said, pulling her mother along with her, and then there was Dad, running toward them, his boat shoes pounding on the wooden slats of the boardwalk. His white shorts and peach, short-sleeved, collared shirt glowed against his burnished skin. The door of their vacation cabin stood open behind him, bright light spilling onto the doorstep and the dark yard.

"There you are!" he called. He sprinted the last few yards between them and threw his arms around her mother.

Her mother gathered Dace into the hug.

"I got us home, Dad," Dace said, her voice muffled by her mother's skirt.

"God, Rowena, what took you so long?" Dad said, pulling back and holding her mother's face in his hands. "I was just about ready to have the park rangers start a search."

"I got one of those ophthalmic migraines down on the beach, and, you know, I can't exactly see when that happens." She closed her eyes and pressed her head into her husband's palm. She opened her eyes. "The only fix, darkness, didn't work. But Dace got us home." Mom stroked Dace's hair, long and sandy colored like Mom's, textured like Dad's.

"Dad, I remembered what you told me about Polaris." Dace tilted her head back to look up at him.

"Good girl," he said, looking down at her and briefly cupping the side of her head. He turned back to gaze into her mother's eyes. "You gave me a scare. Am I going to have to restrict you to base?"

Her mother laughed. "If you must, but first let me go to the Association for Research and Enlightenment, you know, the A.R.E., to find out what jobs are available."

For the second time that evening, her mother clapped her hands over her mouth.

"I did it again!" she said, burying her face in her husband's neck. "I'm not good at keeping secrets."

"We know, don't we, Dace?" Dad grinned at Dace and squeezed her mother in a hug.

When he released her, he took Dace's hand and her mother's and led them back to their rental.

Dad's praise, his enforcement of boundaries and his dry, warm hand clasping hers, with her mother safe beside him, caused relief to flood Dace's limbs, driving out the alarm and dread. Even the worrying prospect of leaving her friends and school in Norfolk to move to Virginia Beach ebbed away, like the retreating tide.

"If you keep working hard to learn more about the stars and lat and long, Dace, they'll always get you to safety." Dad paused in the doorway to let Dace and her mother file into the house. "And safety is family, and family is everything." He closed the door with the three of them inside his temporary castle.

Dace tugged off her Jelly sandals, then trudged up the stairs to the cabin's second floor and her bedroom under the eaves. At the top of the stairs, out of the light, she turned back to say goodnight. Her parents hadn't moved from where they stood facing each other in the front door alcove.

Mom clasped her hands behind his neck, her arms a garland resting on his shoulders "I think I have to correct you on something," she said. "True love is everything. Everything follows from that."

Dad, smiling, gazed silently into her mother's eyes and softened against her, like melting ice cream.

There he goes again, thought Dace.

Whenever Dace's mother both spoke of love and touched Dad, which was often, he not only lost his good posture but also became quiet. Those were her mother's moments of true power over Dad, it seemed to Dace. Was that why true love was everything, Dace wondered, because it had the power to take away another person's speech and ability to stand up straight? She turned away and tiptoed to her room where her lamp in the shape of the planet Saturn, pink with blue stars, glowed softly.

She folded Barbie at the hips then bent her plastic knees and seated her on the edge of the nightstand. The Saturn lamp glowed behind Barbie, and her cheerful smile shone out at Dace. Dace eluded sleep's grasp for as long as she could, then her eyelids drooped heavily and closed.

A pair of orbs like eyes winked on outside the glass of her window under the eaves.

Dace started and woke. She met the orbs' stare. The orbs did not move, nor did she. She could not move; she was paralyzed with fear.

If I scream, Mom and Dad will come, she thought.

She squeezed her eyes shut and screamed. In moments Mom and Dad pounded up the stairs.

Dad shot to her side and scooped her up. He hunkered down into ready position, his center of gravity in his pelvis.

Behind him, Mom leapt forward but he shifted his footing and blocked her. She flew to the other side, and he matched her movement, holding her at bay. She pulled at his shirt.

"Connor, let me have my baby," Mom cried.

"Back," he ordered. He hefted Dace to his right hip and held her tight against him in the crook of his arm, as though she were a rolled-up rug, and swung his left arm out like a gate boom anticipating Mom's movement to that side. He backed out of the room, clutching Dace to his side where Mom had now appeared and tugged at Dace.

At the top of the stairs he swung Dace around so he cradled her and fled down the stairs. Mom in her bare feet followed closely with one hand on the stair rail and the other reaching for Dace and her husband.

He fell heavily onto the couch, still cradling Dace. Mom squeezed next to Dad, and Dad transferred Dace to her waiting arms.

He jumped up, hands on hips. "What happened?"

Mom held Dace tightly and crooned as she pressed her cheek to the top of Dace's head.

"Spindrift man," Dace whispered.

"A man in your room?" Dad barked.

"No, outside my window."

Dad's shoulder's relaxed. "Outside your second-storey window?"

Dace nodded and her hair rubbed against Mom's cheek.

"What did he look like?"

"Big eyes. Glowing. I only saw his eyes."

"I'll be right back," Dad said.

He marched out of the cabin and returned after a few minutes.

"There's no step ladder outside your bedroom window and no marks that there was one," he reported.

"He was there," Dace insisted.

He plunked down beside them. "Oh, Dace, it was a dream," he said.

Mom's head jerked up. "We can't do to her what my parents did to me. They never believed any visit or encounter I had from other worlds. That just messed me up."

Dad shook his head. "Dace did not have a visit or an encounter. If she had, there would have been proof, like marks on the ground from a ladder. When there's proof, we can discuss if it's sufficient and go from there. Besides, why would an alien flying around in his spaceship need a ladder? Right, Dace?" He jiggled her foot.

"Mom?" Dace said, turning her face to look up at Mom.

Mom stared at Dad with narrowed eyes. "Consciousness manifests in many different ways," she said through clenched jaws. "Do you think God or whatever you call that particular being leaves behind evidence when he visits?"

The muscles in Dad's face grew taut. He sat up ramrod

straight on the couch. "We'll have this discussion another time."

"Another time," remarked Mom, shifting her gaze so she stared into space and no longer at Dad. "The time that never comes."

Dace sat up and looked back and forth between her parents. She wasn't sure what they were talking about, but she knew Mom was angry and Dad acted like he did when someone from work called him at home.

Dad's back softened and he leaned against Mom. Dace tapped her toes against his side.

"We should get Dace settled back in bed," he said.

"No!" exclaimed Dace.

Mom squeezed her and again pressed her cheek to her head. "'No' is right," she said, finally looking at Dad. "She can sleep on the couch."

Dad brought down the pillow and blankets from Dace's bedroom, and Mom lay them out on the couch and tucked them around Dace. Mom kissed her forehead, then Dad did too. She turned on her side to watch them walk to their bedroom. Dad had not gone back to his relaxed self. Mom touched his arm.

"Connor?" she asked.

Now he wouldn't look at her.

As Mom followed him into the bedroom, she flicked the switch that controlled the living room lamps and extinguished their glow.

"Light!" called Dace.

Mom paused, her back still to Dace. Then she turned around and flipped the toggle so the lamps came back on. She looked like normal Mom, a bright smile on her face. She blew Dace a kiss and shut the door.

Chapter 1
Beatt

BEATT CAME GENTLY BACK TO his own world when he sensed his watcher, the inner presence that presided over the threshold between outer world and Ssha world. The watcher's presence was brief but always signaled he had crossed the border from one realm into another. Its work done, it softened into its usual nothingness.

Beatt had moved into Ssha world to blur then dissolve his outer-self boundaries, something he did often, but this time it had a purpose: to locate the young woman in a different time and place and continue Mave's work. The young woman's name was Rowena, a name he struggled to pronounce with its watery sounds.

He lifted his tail and shifted to his side on his blanket laid near the fire. It burned low. He pillowed two hands under his cheek and gazed at the glowing embers. He had not been able to fully manifest his outer self in Rowena's time. Mave said she had not either, instead appearing as a white, wispy shape, but Rowena sensed her and understood an intelligence hovered near her. Rowena was the most open human Mave had ever encountered in her travels. It was as though there were no barriers between outer and other worlds for her. Mave had felt hopeful she could transmit Ssha knowledge to her. But the process of moving so often between worlds had done something to her bones, and she was no longer physically able to continue the work. Beatt agreed to take over for her.

He had been so confident he could do it. It had never occurred to him he would not succeed on the first try. It was a new skill, and of their people and those allowed to develop such abilities, much diminished now after the Gigante had moved in, Mave was the only one to master it.

He pushed himself to sitting, sweeping his tail behind him then coiling and binding it around his waist with a tattered strip of cloth he kept for that purpose. He swung his heavy cape around his shoulders.

A pang of loneliness stabbed at his heart. Not so long ago, this room would have been filled with half-and-halfs, semi-divine beings both male and female who had the ability to connect with others' thoughts and communicate. But now they slumbered in the deeper levels with the Ssha, the gentle, giant reptiles, in a sleep they and the Ssha could and likely would remain in forever, their hearts beating so slowly they could not be detected.

It was one thing, it occurred to Beatt, to remain untethered to another when you were surrounded by kin, quite another to maneuver through life almost entirely alone.

Several harvest seasons had passed since the Gigante had come and changed the lives of Dia's residents. They changed those of Apollonoulous, too, but in a less wrenching way, since they had conducted trading business with the former women of hieros house and other residents then married one of the hieros women. From there the Gigante wove themselves into all aspects of the town and its peoples' lives and then simply tightened the weave. For Dia, it was one fell swoop, enabled by the former Executrix of the town, who the Gigante had rewarded with a pig farm of her own outside their settlement.

Beatt's plan had been to use moisovo, mind-speak, to communicate with Mave about his first attempt to obtain her guidance. She lived in Apollonoulous with Tear, a former half-and-half now fully male, as her partner, and Inna, a former hieros woman, her partner Lat and his two children. His heart squeezed, imagining being in the same physical space with people like him. So much could be left unsaid, and so much could simply be said. He craved both that warmth and freedom. The yearning settled it: he would go to Apollonoulous. The Gigante were afraid of the dark and the dead, so Beatt could travel overnight to the cave where Mave and Tear had once lived, and Dia's hieros house women had, before that, once buried the dead. The Gigante employed Dia residents to mine the quartz discovered in the cave, Gigante fear of ghosts overriding their need for control, and one of those workers was Nemmis who had helped Mave and Tear and would help Beatt stay hidden and safe for his day of rest before a night of travel to Apollonoulous.

He tied the fabric strings on his buskins and secured his long, dark hair at the nape of his neck with another fabric scrap. Beatt had torn these scraps from the few blankets the half-and-halfs had left behind in their hurry to descend into the deepest parts of the cave with the Ssha.

He rose and gathered several handfuls of dried berries and tubers from his supply nook. Mave had told him her body lagged when she moved into other times; it took time for hunger and monthly bleeding to return, though Beatt would not have to worry about the latter. By the time he reached Mave in Apollonoulous in the two nights of walking it required, he might be ready to eat a full meal.

He shouldered the cloth bag of his food and stood at the cave entrance. Thorny brambles crisscrossed the opening. He imagined himself slipping easily through the barbed tunnel. He stepped confidentially into the nettles. He yelped in pain and jumped back. He had banged his forehead on the burr. He touched his finger to his brow and examined it—no blood—just surface scratches.

Not a good sign, he thought. *Either the brambles know something I don't know or I'm losing my abilities.*

He aligned his mind with the Sshas', what little he could access in their stasis. His consciousness softened and his thinking slowed. Thoughts ebbed and dispersed. The "I" of him receded, and when that I was no more, he fell forward into the thicket. The thicket softened, and Beatt stepped through.

There was a price to move into worlds far removed from their own. While Mave understood the cost to her—worn-down bones, ever-present pain—Beatt was only just discovering hints as to what his might be.

Chapter 2
A Girl Who Can't Say No

IN THE OFFICES OF THEY Who Ride, her father's GPS fleet tracking development company, Dace sat in a sea of gray-walled cubes. Co-workers populated the other cubes, but they were as quiet as Dace, and the only sound was the tapping of the keyboards. The overhead lights were off and natural light filtered in through the solitary skylight, recreating for the senses the inside of a fighter jet cockpit. Each cube had one fluorescent tube installed underneath the cabinet, casting a bluish light on the work surface but leaving the rest of the area in dusky light, the gloam of other worlds, her mother's contribution to the office décor.

Dace sat as still as a mannequin; only her fingers were alive, flying and trilling over the keyboard. With one earbud in, the other dangling, her one ear alert to the outside world, she transcribed the notes she'd taken at the Monday morning scrum meeting with the API developers. Lat, long, she chanted to herself, her inner chorus that kept her in line with her ideal self: always be perfect, always be working.

Meladee's head appeared above her cube wall. The spiky, goldenrod tips of her friend's short, lavender hair framed her face like the sun's rays.

"Got an outfit picked out for your date tonight?" she whispered.

A burr of anxiety churned in Dace's stomach. She raised one finger and found a good stopping place in the audio recording. She didn't want to go on this second date with Jonah, a guy she'd met with Meladee last month at a Bahama Breeze happy hour. Meladee had pushed the two of them together then ducked out before Dace could stop her. Jonah was a nice enough guy but wore his shoulder-length hair combed back in a lion's mane, which would never pass muster with Dad. Dace and Jonah had gone out once, to see "Apocalypse Now: Final Cut" at the Naro, a movie which Jonah loved but her dad would hate. She'd have to take sides. *Could I do that?* she thought. *Maybe.* She was attracted to Jonah and especially his hair, imagining being under him during sex and his hair falling and enclosing the two of them like curtains. Since Meladee had been hired she was closer than she'd ever been to acting and behaving ways different from her usual constrained habits. At 27, Dace hovered between breaking out of her old ways of doing things and settling for good into what was a well-worn groove of bittersweet loneliness. She spent most Saturday nights with her parents, watching a movie and eating popcorn, which Mom popped on the stove the old-fashioned way and dusted with brewer's yeast. On Sundays, Dace brought bagels and cream cheese and read the papers with her parents. On holidays, Dace packed a small bag and spent several days with them.

She tapped pause. "Got it right here," she whispered to Meladee, and reached for the Tiger Mist bag under her desk. She pulled it out and grimaced at the crinkling sound of the plastic bag as she started to open it. She cautiously placed it back on the floor. "You'll have to take my word for what's inside," she said quietly, "white bandage skirt and white V-neck t-shirt."

"Shoes?" Meladee asked.

Dace peered underneath the desk as though a pair of date shoes might magically appear. "Guess I forgot about shoes." She swiveled in her chair and lifted one foot to display her black Oxford lace-up. "Will these do?"

Meladee came around to the opening to Dace's cube. Her oversized, white-collared shirt was cinched at the waist with a velvet ruby belt, and with it she paired a black spandex mini skirt. She studied Dace, tilting her head and pulling on the ends of her spiky hair. "Hm, librarian shoes can strike a certain note, but nah, I think they're too heavy for the outfit." She kept her voice low. "Do you have sneakers?"

Dace shook her head.

"The last person in America not to own a pair of sneakers," Meladee said, smiling. "What size do you wear?"

"Six."

"I'll go out at lunch and find you a pair. Hey, would that make you my client? I can add that to the resume I'm building for life coach jobs. Data analysis isn't exactly a segue to the world of helping people meet their potential." Meladee paused. "Have you tried what I suggested, recording yourself talking then watching yourself?"

"Please don't make me do that," Dace said.

Meladee yelped in laughter then clapped her hand over her mouth. "Whoops," she whispered. "Didn't mean to laugh. You don't have to do anything you don't want to do. Like I have that kind of power!"

"It's okay," Dace assured her in hushed tones.

A wave of something warm floated toward Dace like an

airplane's contrail, which Dace recognized as Dad's energy. "Mr. Banks is on his way up the stairs."

Meladee pressed her palms together at heart level. "Blessings on your freaky skills," she said.

The beam of Dad's energy increased in intensity. She inclined her head toward the office front door. "Incoming."

Over the cube wall, Dace could see the office door opening. Dace slipped in her earbuds and returned to her work.

Meladee reached over Dace's cube wall for a pad of Post-Its. She wrote furiously as the soothing flow of technical terminology wash over Dace. Lat, long, lat, long, her own personal lullaby.

Meladee slapped the Post-It against the fabric cube wall directly in front of Dace, then sped off. Dace glanced at the note. "Look forward to receiving your new date shoes after lunch. No cancelling this time! Love, Meladee."

Dace was already slipping into her transcription trance. Robotically, she turned back to her screen. Her five senses receded, and her conscious self sank like a plumb bob. Her sense of an "I" disappeared.

Dad appeared and lightly tapped his knuckles on top of the cube wall.

"Miss Banks," he said, his tenor voice low.

Dace quickly surfaced. She paused the recording and looked up. "Yes, sir?"

Dad's dusky face was set and serious. "I'm assigning you to scribe for Mr. Diggle during these remaining phases of the GEOV project."

"All right," Dace said to her father but to herself thought, *Oh, no*. She guessed they'd lost the temp who had been working on this project. This was the third temp they'd lost in the past three months. Her father ran his business like he ran his family: adherence to the established rules and codes of conduct, which earned his loyalty and a secure place. His partner, Captain Cabassa, who Dace called Uncle Cab, with whom he'd started They Who Ride, had a decidedly different style and couldn't work like that. He left after two years. Sometimes new hires left much sooner, and temps… well, they lived up to their name when they came to work at They Who Ride. The rules and rigidity were too much for most.

His face remained dispassionate. "I'll reassign whatever you're working on. Shadow Diggle for the duration, on base or off. Gather and document every word he says. Where Dibble goes, you go."

"Yes, sir," Dace said. "Is Mr. Dibble coming onsite today?"

Dad nodded curtly. "I told him he'd better live up to his title, Idea Innovator. Meeting in ten. His partner will be here too, the engineer who determines initial feasibility of Dibble's ideas, Mr.—" He cast his eyes skyward, as though that would jolt his memory. "Ricci," he said, snapping his fingers, "Jack Ricci."

Dace's heart jumped at the sound of his name. Just like the first time she met him, her body responded, vibrating like a tuning fork. She couldn't speak.

"Dibble had better be close to showing results," Dad continued. "Our team project manager at Seek-Vee tells me we're behind on the timeline and I've got HSIN and FBI expecting results." Dad tapped on the metal covering of her cube wall. "Five minutes," he said, "then we'll all convene." He pivoted on his heel and trod in a near-march down the hall to his office.

Dace shook her head, as though to clear it. "Lat, long, lat, long," she whispered.

Brandon Dibble materialized out of the shadows, his head bent to his phone. He was a tall, lanky man with chin-length straight hair parted down the center, Anna Wintour without the bangs, and black square spectacles. He looked up from his phone. "Dace," he said. He rested his arms on the top of her cube wall and thumbed his device. "Uh, sorry, Miss Banks."

Dace cleared her throat. "I understand I'll be taking over as your scribe."

Brandon bobbed his chin in a nod. "Ready when you are," he said. "Actually, I'm working on a thought experiment about harnessing electricity from the earth's rotation. You're familiar with thought experiments, right?"

"Yes, conducting experiments using your imagination."

"I would say creating a vision mentally, but yeah what you said works."

Without raising his head, he shuffled back and leaned against the opposite cube wall, as though waiting for a bus.

Where Dad's essence was a contrail, Ricci's was the tendril of the cirrus wafting toward her. Filaments snaked toward her, and her body tingled as though lightning were about to strike. A few moments later the front door opened, and Jack Ricci approached. He focused on Brandon slouching against the wall with his face buried in his phone.

Jack Ricci was about Dad's height—medium, like a good bear, her dad always said—but where Dad was slender like a Kennedy, Ricci was built like a wrestler, with broad shoulders and a barrel torso. He wore a black suit made of fabric so luxurious even from several feet away Dace could see the fabric's strength and softness in the weave. His sky-blue tie lay against a white shirt. He had a full head of dark hair with crisply-trimmed sideburns tinged with platinum. He glanced at Dace, the dim light reflecting off the lenses of his wire-rim spectacles so that his brown eyes seemed to flash, as he paused at Brandon's side.

"Miss Banks," he said. He dipped his chin in the slightest of nods. His eyes behind his spectacles gave away nothing.

The usual feathery brush at her nape was replaced by the flick of a horse's tail, a caress with power and strength. She opened her mouth to answer his greeting but nothing came out.

He turned away and spoke to Brandon.

Damn it, she thought, *where are my words?*

"Okay, see you in a minute," Brandon said.

Ricci departed down the same hall Dad had traveled.

Brandon lingered. "Ready to scribe?" he asked, raising his head to look at Dace.

At that moment, Meladee charged up to the opening of Dace's cube. Brandon appeared star-struck, as though his fantasy woman had come to life. Meladee ignored him. She looked at the hall Dad and Jack Ricci had traveled down as though checking to be sure the coast was clear.

"Coffee?" she asked Dace in a hushed voice.

"Miss Gomez, you know our consultant, Mr. Brandon Dibble?" Dace said.

Brandon appeared transfixed. His arm holding his phone hung limply at his side. Meladee spun toward him and said quickly, "Nice to meet you," then pivoted back to Dace.

"Come on, clock's ticking," Meladee said. "These damn ten-minute breaks your dad allows us are killing me. He makes us sign in and out of the time-tracking software, but I guess you know that. You will too, new guy," she finished, looking briefly at Brandon.

"No timecards for Mr. Dibble. He's a consultant," Dace said, smiling. "He and his partner—" Words failed her.

"Do you get domestic partner benefits when you consult?" Meladee asked him.

"No, no, no, Ricci's not that kind of partner," Brandon said.

"We went to school together, then we started doing these gigs together. That kind of partner. A business partner."

"Whatever kind of couple you are, it's totally fine." Meladee looked down, checking her phone. "Did you say Ricci? Hm, Ricci." She tapped her chin. Realization dawned. "*That* Ricci?" she asked Dace.

Dace widened her eyes, pursed her lips, and shook her head.

"We are so not like any kind of couple," Brandon said, pressing his fingers to his brow. "In fact, he was married to my sister. That's how not coupled we are." Brandon stepped from foot to foot.

Josh and Chad, two They Who Ride developers working on the GEOV project, tromped by. Both wore checked collared shirts with long sleeves rolled up to their respective elbows, Josh in navy blue, Chad in red. As they passed Dace's cube, Josh rapped his knuckles on her cube. "Two minutes, Icy," he said in a low whisper.

He and Chad continued down the hall, laughing under their breath. Dace's face burned.

"Ignore those idiots," Meladee said quietly to Dace.

A ding sounded on Dace's machine. "I can't do coffee," she said to Meladee. "Meeting in two."

Meladee sighed. She turned to Brandon. "All right, new guy, how about you?"

Brandon's jaw dropped.

"Sorry, he can't," Dace said.

He scratched his cheek. "I can't?"

Dace shook her head. "Meeting's about to start, and you're a required attendee." She gathered her folio and power cord. "The meeting's in the Jeannie Leavitt conference room. Straight down that hall." She pointed. "You go ahead, and I'll be right there."

When Brandon didn't move, Dace stepped out of her cube

and again pointed toward the conference room where the meeting would be held. "That way," she said. "Follow Josh and Chad."

Brandon obeyed. He headed down the hall and rubbed the back of his neck as he went.

Meladee rested her elbows on Dace's cube wall and watched with a little smile on her face.

"How do you do it?" Dace asked in a low voice.

Meladee shrugged. "Guys like it when you're mean," she said in an equally quiet voice. "So much for a coffee break." She started down a path between cubes leading to hers then stopped and doubled back. "Hey, the testing your dad needs volunteers for, for the scenario actors, is that for the new app this Dibble guy is developing?"

"You aren't going to volunteer just to torture him, are you?" Dace said under her breath while she checked her phone for the time. Dad didn't tolerate lateness in himself or any of his employees, including family.

"Maybe, maybe not," Meladee whispered and sauntered away, waving her fingers at Dace.

Dace walked quickly down the narrow aisle to the meeting room.

Brandon hovered outside, like a moth unsure of its attraction to light. Dace sidled past him into the room, nodding so that he followed. Her eyes went immediately to Ricci sitting in profile at the end of the table. His cirrus essence snaked toward her, and something lit up deep within her. Thankful her father held him absorbed in a whispered conversation, Dace clutched her folio to her pounding heart. She found a seat quickly on Chad and Josh's side of the table, near the door. This kept Ricci barely visible beyond the two developers' heads.

Could anything be worse than being attracted to a

consultant and risking that business relationship? *Yes*, she answered herself as she opened her folio. *Acting on it.*

Brandon looked back and forth between Ricci and her dad and Josh and Chad before he pulled out a chair opposite the two developers. They each flicked a glance at Brandon as he seated himself, then looked back down at their laptops opened on the table. Brandon mirrored them, laying his tablet flat on the table, tapping it, then peering at it.

"Everyone," Dad said, "let's get started. This meeting is about a layered view we're creating for road cameras in the US, to be used by Seek-Vee, a camera asset management company for several fleet management companies. Because of their connections with federal agencies, we now have two of those agencies interested in the project. All parties want the layered view the APIs would allow—geography, people, weather--with the aim of a more complete driving condition report for the fleet management companies and surveillance for the feds. A real-time layered view would allow computerized selection of the best route given unexpected conditions due to weather or geo-political events. Josh and Chad are working on the GIS APIs."

The developers dipped their head without looking up from their devices.

"We've brought Mr. Dibley in," Dad continued, "to create the actual app, called GEOV, which will use APIs to ingest lat and long and a database of geographical images and location services. In addition, Mr. Dibley will also create the API that will complete the view: individual profiles. The data source for these can either be users self-identifying or an aggregated view of an individual compiled from public social media and web activity."

Dace sat still as a figurine on a shelf, her only movement her fingers flying over the keyboard, inputting every word.

Some experienced scribes said they could simultaneously input spoken words and let their focus shift to another subject, but this was not the case with Dace. She had to keep her mind focused on herself as an empty vessel, no longer a person, to be filled with information that her fingers found corresponding symbols for on her keyboard.

"What if someone doesn't use the web?" Josh asked.

"We use publicly available databases like birth and death," Brandon said. "Unless someone is 300 years old, we'll find him. However, we've got some unconventional methods of fleshing out the individual's identity." Brandon paused. "Mr. Banks, can I assume we're all under the same confidentiality agreement?"

Dad nodded. "You can. Go ahead."

"Each person has a measurable electromagnetic field," Brandon continued. "The heart generates the largest electromagnetic field in the body. These fields are coded and transmit that information throughout the body. The fields also have markers that link up to other characteristics we can infer from the aggregated data."

Dace's eyelids drooped as the words poured into her and her fingers flew.

"The cameras use a radio signal to measure a person's electromagnetic field created by their heart, then incorporates that data into the aggregated data for a comprehensive picture of the person. Then the app matches that up to actual individuals for what we believe will be a ninety percent or better match."

"Auras," Ricci said.

Dace's head shot up. "Aura" was a term her mother used but one Dace had never heard used in any business context. As though to check the veracity of what she had heard, she turned to look at Ricci. His supercooled gaze swept from her dad down the table, apparently gauging the effect of his term on the group. When he looked directly at her, she felt, improbably, that he took in what she was thinking. He acknowledged her with a slight nod and smile which faded as soon as Josh got in the way. He had folded his arms across his chest, and leaned back in his chair, blocking her from Ricci's gaze.

"'Auras are what lay people call this electromagnetic field,' Ricci continued. "But you don't need mystical powers to measure them. Just the right technology, including a very strong signal, and Brandon's—Mr. Dibley's—app and the APIs."

Brandon leaned forward as though to speak. She glanced at Ricci. He caught Brandon's eye and moved his head side to side, signaling "No." He briefly touched his index finger to his lips.

Dace felt the warmth of his finger on her own lips. Her fingers lost their contact with the keyboard, and she sat back in her chair.

"Is this a good time to show everyone how this will work?" asked Dace's father, looking back and forth between Ricci and Brandon who both nodded.

Dace snapped forward. She pressed her lips together tightly until the pain dispelled the feelings of warmth and cut the connection to the wisps of Ricci's essence snaking like cirrus threads around her. She went back into her transcription trance, keying rapidly, capturing everything that was said, trying to ignore the anxiety whirring in her stomach. Somehow she would have to find a way to capture those words of Ricci's she missed when her transcription trance lapsed.

Dad inserted a cable into his laptop and pointed a remote control at a projector installed on the ceiling. The image projected on the blank wall. Camera views snapped into a grid, locking against each other, forming an L-shape.

"Most of you are familiar with the MACC view," he said. "Only you'll see near-real-time views and feeds from the cameras on a driver's route. Then we'll bring in the other datasets, create layers such as topography with the GIS software. Finally, with Mr. Dibble's help, we'll have profiles from both known and unknown individuals in the vicinity. Mr. Dibble, can you give us a report on your progress and any issues you've encountered?"

Brandon smoothed his hand over his hair at the crown, already a velvety sheet. "I've completed the ingestion of They Who Ride's APIs created by your developers There were a few bugs in the first iteration, and now all of those have been fixed. I've completed the work for the profiles, known and aggregated or unknown, ingested those APIs and all the others into GEOV and am ready to test."

"No issues?" Josh asked.

Dace caught the hooded glance Brandon cast at Ricci.

"We're working on a solution for an external energy source," Ricci said.

Brandon nervously tapped his fingers.

"Meaning?" Dad asked.

"The GEOV app will live on the camera servers," Ricci continued, "but the actual device that measures human electromagnetic energy will need to be mounted with the cameras. The cameras are battery powered and the batteries are solar chargeable due to the design. The batteries in the control panel of the device, called a SQUID-based magnetometer, are not solar chargeable due to design as well, but I'd say it's a defect, not a feature. The company that makes the magnetometer is working on the issue, though they call it an enhancement request. Until they come up with a solution, we run the risk of the batteries running down and having no way to replace them. Obviously, we would have a process in place to manually replace them, but there's always the what-if risk: what if Plan B fails? To mitigate that risk, we're working on Plan C, another energy source."

"We need the GEOV app ready to test this week if we're going to stay on schedule," Josh said, leaning back and crossing his arms.

Brandon again nervously smoothed his mane. He addressed Dace's father: "Connor, we'll be ready. We *are* ready. We can test day after tomorrow. I've reserved my usual testing location."

At the sound of her father's given name, Josh and Chad froze as though they were playing statue. Dace's chest tightened in the silence that followed. Brandon had breached protocol.

"Very good," Dad finally said, breaking the silence in the room.

Dace let out the exhale she was holding, and Josh and Chad resumed tapping their devices.

"We'll have our in-house scenario actors lined up end of day today," Dad said. "Meeting adjourned."

Dad turned to Brandon, then Ricci. "Would you both stay? And Miss Banks, you too. Mr. Jones, Mr. Greening, would you come back in ten and work with Mr. Dibble to be sure he's got all the access he needs for the onsite scenario testing?"

"Yes, Mr. Banks," Chad and Josh said in unison, then rose and left the room.

Dace's father rose and closed the door, then returned to his seat. "Miss Banks, would you send both Mr. Dibble and Mr. Ricci a reminder link to our in-office demeanor and other office policies?" Dace nodded and continued typing. "I know it's not everyone's cup of tea, but we're mister and miz around here. Honorific, or title, then last name. Old Navy habit. One that dies hard." He looked levelly at Brandon then Ricci. "We run a tight ship around here. Doesn't work for everyone. But for those it does, and those who stay with us, we consider family."

Ricci nodded. "Understood," he said. "That's how I prefer it."

"Very good," her dad said to Ricci, with a crisp nod of his head.

Both Dad and Ricci looked at Brandon who took another swipe down the back of his head. "Uh, yeah, for sure. Yes. Definitely. Sir. Mister. Mister Banks." Brandon blushed furiously, the blood rising from the base of his neck. His eyes were downcast.

Dad rose. Dace knew silence was never neutral with him but it wasn't damning; it just meant he'd given you a temporary reprieve and a chance to do better next time.

Dad pushed in his chair. "Mr. Jones and Mr. Greening should be back in a minute to work with Brandon on access. Dace, will you work with Mr. Dibble and Mr. Ricci on any of the terminology? Share the glossary we've got on the current project site."

Ricci stood and smiled at Dace. "I'll see how far I can get with Google," he said and followed Dad out of the room.

The emotional warmth of Ricci's smile entered her like tendrils of wispy clouds which then broke loose inside her mind and heart. The filaments spread throughout her body, delicately touching all the most sensitive spots.

The sensation abruptly ended when her father turned back to face Dace and Brandon. The surprise of his change in routine—he never reentered a meeting he'd left—brought Dace back to the hard chair and the bright lights.

"Of course, when we're outside work hours, we use each

other's first names," Dad said to Brandon with a smile that to Dace seemed pasted on. "So, if we run into each other, say, at the grocery store, don't be surprised if I say, 'Hi, Bibble'!"

Brandon's eyes opened wide in confusion. He looked at Dace.

"Uh, Mr. Banks," Dace began.

Dad glanced down then back up. His jaw tightened. "My apologies. I would say, 'Hi, Dandon'."

Brandon's brow furrowed in consternation. "Okay," he said slowly.

Dad's mouth opened to speak but then he snapped it shut, spun on his heel and departed the room at a smart clip.

Brandon sank into his chair and stared at his screen. Dace stared at hers, too, her emotions jerked in another direction by the shock of hearing Dad's verbal blunder, a thing she'd never heard come out of his mouth. He wasn't having a stroke, was he? she wondered. She leaned over her computer and frantically looked up "stroke symptoms."

"Miss Banks," Chad said, tapping the table in front of her machine.

Her head snapped up.

Chad nodded in the direction of the door. Dad stood there, beckoning for Dace to join him.

"What is it, Mr. Banks?" she asked when she stood with him just outside the conference room.

He motioned for her to follow him down the hall, to the end where the doors led only to the rarely used stairs.

"Are you all right?" Dace asked him quietly.

"I'm fine," he said. "But Mom's not. She's not feeling well and can't go to a practice descent of Jez' tonight at Oblation Station. You remember Jez?"

Dace nodded mutely. Jez was all Mom could talk about a few weeks back. Mom had met both Jez and the head oblate, Agnes, when she'd dropped off her job application at Oblation Station, but it was only Jez she could talk about. Jez told her about the descents she ran at the Station, designed to help people access other realms, as Mom, glowing, told Dad and Dace that night at dinner. Ecstatic at finding a kindred spirit, Mom offered to help Jez with the testing of the descents, and Jez promised to help Mom get a job at the Station. Mom felt meeting Jez was meant to be. In the meantime, *The Virginian-Pilot* had run an article about Jez' descents last week and described the transition of the convent of contemplative Sisters to a non-secular retreat center. Moore Electric bought the convent which was dying from lack of new prospects. The image of Jez that accompanied the article suggested to Dace a woman who knew how to get noticed: tousled black hair, lush, red lips, eyes ringed in kohl, a secretive smile playing on her lips. Jez didn't strike Dace as the guide to other worlds, at least not those designed to elevate one's spirit life.

"I don't know if Jez will be there but one of her descenders will," Dad continued. "Mom has got her heart set on changing jobs from the A.R.E. to across the street at the Station. She feels strongly if she helps Jez, Jez will help her get the job. Would you go in Mom's place?"

Dace's heart sank. Her mother loved the A.R.E. for the work it did, from the research into altered states of consciousness to the benefits of the health center. However, in all the years she had been here, Mom had tried but failed to get a job outside of the retail shop at the center.

Dad's voice dropped down to a whisper. "I'm not impressed with Jez either," he said, correctly interpreting Dace's silence, "but she's harmless. She's no more a potential threat than your mom. Will you? Help Mom out? I'd rather see her work at a retreat center than the gift shop of the A.R.E."

Dace said nothing.

"I want your mother safe, not with people who encourage her imaginings but with those whose profession requires kindness. At Oblation Station she'd be with nuns."

"Former nuns," Dace noted dully, knowing she had to do what he asked and help keep mom safe. "If it matters, now they're called 'oblates'."

The stairwell door flew open, and Meladee charged out then reared back to avoid ramming into her boss. "'Scuze me, Mr. Banks," she said. She ducked quickly behind him and held up her bulky white bag for Dace to see then sped down the hall.

"The main thing is," Dad said, his voice low, "there's not going to be any mumbo-jumbo business if former nuns are around."

"Dad, Jez Bell is the queen of mumbo-jumbo," Dace said. "Have you been following the stories in *The Pilot* and on social media about her 'descents'? She says they allow you to pass into the void and through to other worlds."

The phone he held in his hand sounded. He glanced at the display then let his arm fall back to his side. "You know I don't do social media. But I did see the article." His phone buzzed again. "I have to go," he said. "Be my astonishing daughter." He turned before she could speak and departed down the hall with his phone pressed to his ear.

"But I have a date," she called weakly to his retreating back.

He turned the corner into the cluster of cubes that led to his office.

She re-worked the schedule in her mind. If she wore her date outfit to the descent, whatever that actually involved, and said she had to leave early, she could just make it to Bahama Breeze for the last 30 minutes of happy hour and hope that Jonah waited.

Or she could cancel, but that would be the second time she'd cancelled with Jonah. If he were like the other fellows she'd occasionally dated, cancelling twice would mean he wouldn't try a third time. The image of Meladee grinning and holding up the large white bag flashed through her mind. She didn't care about losing Jonah and his meager boyfriend potential but she did care about disappointing Meladee. But disappoint her dad? That she could not do. She couldn't imagine getting over doing something like that.

Damn that Jez, Dace thought, *damn me.*

Chapter 3
Beatt Seeks Guidance at Apollonoulous

BEATT NEARED THE BORDER OF Apollonoulous. An uneventful day of sleep in Mave and Tear's former cave home had left him refreshed. Nemesis had concocted a story of restless spirits in the cave which, when she reported to the Gigante who drove the cart of workers to the mountain, caused him to harness the horse, hook up the cart, and from his driver's seat direct the horse a good distance away from the mountain. The workers, formerly free citizens of Dia, picked the olives and those in the cave mining the quartz dug as quietly as possible so Beatt could sleep.

The dark was still deep though it was not long before the horizon would light to shadowed lavender as the sun made its way up.

Beatt surveyed the town's dim outlines. It was not much bigger than when the hieros house women had governed from their large, central pod. The surrounding, smaller pods still stood, but tall tents were erected on the side that faced the sea and the skeletons of large, square structures were next to the tents. Beyond them, another skeleton of a structure, this one with a roof that rose into a peak.

Nemmis had told him to enter on the side opposite the sea. The Gigante kept watch only on the sea side. They were confident they had subdued Dia sufficiently to not worry there would be an uprising, or at least this was Nemmis' theory. The people of Dia were not accustomed to a combative way of life. They preferred freedom, and the transition had been hard, but many like Nemmis and the olive pickers and quartz miners had found ways to feel free in their new condition. In truth, said Nemmis, the hieros house women had their own way of constraining the people of Dia, though their daily lives were mostly their own. Their nights, of course, were of exquisite freedom when the hieros house women led them in void rituals. But even so, participation was required for everyone; well, except Mave.

Mave, Beatt sent out in mind-verse.

Here, came the response like a heartbeat. A tiny, second response followed. It too felt like a heart's rhythm.

Two women named Mave? pondered Beatt. *If so, they feel to be in the same place.*

The rising sun added a layer of yellow to the horizon.

He set off toward the cluster of small pods where in the now purple-tinged gray light rows of rope were strung between poles. Some had cloths draped over them, drying.

Here, came again the beat of thought, followed by its muted echo.

Beatt's body complied and veered toward the lines strung between the poles and then just beyond them, where Mave stood with a bucket at the well. Beast pushed up against her, a brace.

She did not turn when he approached. He hunched, as Nemmis had instructed him, and hung his head as he joined her at the well.

She lowered the wooden bucket into the well then pulled it back up with muffled grunts of effort.

Beatt extended his hands to take the bucket's rope. Mave shook her head and nodded toward the tents on the sea side and then toward the large, center pod where the Gigante Thras and Poulx, former head of hieros house, now lived. Beatt withdrew his hands.

Beast jumped on the well's edge. It found purchase wedging its hindquarters between the well and Mave's belly. Cushioned, Mave rest her forearms on beast and hoisted the bucket up with her swollen, knobby hands. Bracing herself against Beast, she hauled the bucket off the edge and held it with two hands.

Beast nudged her. She looked down at it, and it took the bucket rim gently in its teeth and tugged.

Mave smiled and shook her head. She raised her head and whispered, "Beast doesn't know it's invisible to most, certainly all the Gigante. I'd cause big trouble if anyone saw a bucket of water floating along next to me."

She set the bucket back on the well's edge and leaned heavily against Beast.

"Would there be trouble if I carried it?" asked Beatt in a voice as soft as hers.

"No, but I'm determined to do what needs to be done no matter the pain. If I don't...." Her voice trailed off.

Beast rubbed its head against her. She stroked its head. "I wouldn't need Beast, for one thing, if I stopped doing anything that caused pain, because everything causes pain. Need conjures Beast and others of its kind."

Shouts came from the tents. Beatt jumped.

"Not to worry," Mave said. "That's how the Gigante start the day. Let's go." She again took the bucket in her two hands and, with Beast bracing her, took small, labored steps away from the well.

Beatt, still stooped with his head bowed, followed Mave on the short walk to a pod.

Inna opened the pod door as they stepped up to it.

"Finally," she said, taking the bucket from Mave. "In, quickly."

Inna set the bucket down as Mave settled herself by the glowing embers of the fire. Beast's faint outline dissolved.

Beatt sat down on one of several stools near the fire. Inna poured half of the bucket's water into another bucket, then scooped out two cupfuls and handed one to Mave then Beatt. Inna settled on a stool between Mave and Beatt.

Beatt drank the cool water and unfurled from his hunch. He relaxed in the warmth and the presence of Mave and Inna.

This is all I need, he thought. *Joined in silence with others like me. And a chance to light when the sun rises.*

"We have a few minutes until the sun crests the horizon," Mave said. "If you can make your lighting look like a stretch after waking, it should be safe enough."

"Start, Mave," Inna said. "Lat and his children are still asleep. I don't want them to see Beatt." She glanced at Beatt. "I'm sorry, Beatt, but it's just not safe. The first thing they'll notice is your abnormally big middle, and they'll want to know why it's so. Tear won't be back from his job at the docks until tonight, and we're vulnerable until he's here."

"He?" Beatt asked.

"Yes, Tear is fully and forever 'he' now," Mave answered. "At least I think irreversibly. He reverted back to his half-and-half self when the Ssha returned him to me after I could no longer take their message into other times, but once we settled here in Apollonoulous our need required him to become a he again."

"Your need?"

Mave grimaced and looked at Inna.

"Our need to eat and clothe ourselves," Inna said. "Everyone who needs those things works. Mave and I run a laundry, Lat looks after his children, and Tear works down at the docks." Inna slapped both palms on her thighs. "Beatt, why don't you proceed with asking Mave what you need to know about the travelling into other times."

Beatt nodded and took another sip of water, giving himself a moment to contain the sadness at the loss of Tear's half-and-half nature. "Are the humans always so frightened by us?"

"From what I could tell, they didn't think of me as another being like them. And, in truth, I am like them; my Ssha blood is half of what yours and my mother's is, and you are both one-half Ssha. Too, my mother never indicated our lineage, so until you came into my life not so long ago, I believed myself to be exactly like all the people of Dia, only too frightened by the dark and the void rituals to ever take part."

"What did those you visited think of you?" Inna asked.

"There was no 'me' to them. Many seemed to have no awareness of me. Some seemed to sense me. When they did, they erupted out of sleep and either screamed or fled to the others in their dwellings. I would have followed them but found the squareness of their structures and blinding light sources disorienting. Instead of one fire they had many small fires, and high up. By the time I was finding my way toward those I was visiting, their fear dissolved the possible connection."

"What about those who weren't so afraid?"

The sun rose above the horizon. Its rays shone through the narrow spaces between the door and the pod walls. Beatt shifted his stool to be aligned with a slanting ray. He held up the arm nearest the door, palm out and up. This would have to do for the day's lighting. Both Mave and Inna sat quietly. When Beatt's arm slowly dropped and he held his glowing palm to his chest, Mave spoke.

"There were a few moments where they seemed stunned but not yet overcome by fear. That gave them time to see me but I came through only as a pale, tiny being. When I looked down at myself, my dun-colored shift seemed to have melded to me, like a second skin. When the shock wore off, the fear set in. Only one, the one I told you about, named Rowena, remained in that in-between state long enough for me to connect with her using mind-verse. Just once I spoke my full name, Mavealeph, but I could tell the sound didn't come out right. She never relaxed during these visits. Her body remained rigid, her eyes wide. How to not cause them fear?"

"I found Rowena," Beatt said. "At the sea's edge. I felt certain she could see me. She looked directly at me. Another human stood next to her, taller, older."

Mave cocked her head. "How tall? Gigante tall?"

He shook his head. "Tall like the Gigante priests. Rowena was shorter, like you or Inna, but I don't know what that means given I was in a different time and place."

Mave considered. "Rowena wasn't that small when I was visiting her. She was closer to Gigante priest height, but still shorter. She was a young woman, or at least I sensed she was."

Silence fell as each receded into their own thoughts.

"Can we assume if I was pulled there, that was Rowena, but perhaps at a younger age?"

"I can't say with any certainty, but I think we have to," said Mave. "There's no other way to make sense of it. If you did find Rowena at a younger age, I wonder if there's a way to...."

"To?" Inna prodded.

"I was going to say 'wait until she's older,' but that doesn't make sense. We don't seem to have control over the timing, so what does 'wait' even mean?"

Again silence fell.

"Like yours, my body did not fully manifest. I was sparkly, like Beast," Beatt offered.

"Hm," Mave said, "perhaps there must be mutual need to be seen and heard as we are, at least in ways they understand?"

"Possibly. When I was drawn to Rowena's dwelling, where another was, a man, and was able to send my consciousness to where I felt she was, high above in the dwelling, she woke and screamed, which brought the other two. They treated her as though something terrible had happened. The man gathered her up, and he and the woman, partners, they seemed. I sent my consciousness in to follow them, but the descent from the height was dizzying. My ability to be in that time faltered, but I stayed present long enough to watch the two sit with Rowena for a while on some sort of long bench covered in what looked like layer upon layer of blankets. And yes, they had the same blinding light sources, several of them. Eventually the two went into another room and the light sources went out then came back on. That was too much for me, and that overcame Ssha need to work with humans to receive their message."

"It always comes back to the body," Mave murmured. "The body is the gatekeeper. And the body always ends. Then we end."

Inna moved to her side and sat beside her. "Is the pain very bad?"

"Always bad, but I'm getting used to it."

"We'll find a healer who knows how to treat this."

"A healer who treats the effects of moving back and forth

between different times and places, the shock of encountering different worlds, smells and sights, being called and returned by the potential of others and the need of the Ssha? Even if we could find such a healer, and that would be unlikely given most have followed Turnip's example and portray themselves as harmless fools, they wouldn't understand the words we use to describe the experience. We're the only the people who know of this."

Mave sagged. Inna lightly draped a woven shawl around her shoulders, then knelt at her feet. She took each calloused foot in her hands and held them, warming them.

"I wish I'd been a member of hieros house long enough to learn more," Inna said. "I was just beginning when the Gigante arrived on Apollonoulous' shores. I would break the rule and tell what I know, only I don't know anything."

"Anta?" asked Beatt.

Mave shook her head. "We tried. The Gigante don't allow the House of Hor women any freedoms beyond overseeing the laundry near their pods. They want them where they can find them when they need them."

Tinkling bells rang outside the door.

"Turnip," explained Inna. "We asked for his help. He's arranged a safe place for you to rest today so you can make the return journey tonight." She hesitated, looking down.

"You'll have to appear as a slave," Mave said. "Turnip's slave, which makes you the lowest of the low, one rung below the fool of two towns. If you're collared, the Gigante assume you're subdued and not worth bothering about."

Rustling sounds came from the other room. Small voices chirped sleepily, and a lower voice murmured.

Inna shot to standing. "The children."

The door opened a crack, and in popped the conical hat with its bells then Turnip's head. His practiced leer turned serious. Beatt rose.

"Hurry," Inna said, "I'll keep the children in the other room with me and Lat. They'll all be hungry, so I won't be able to hold them for long."

Turnip stepped in and looped a strand of woven hemp around Beatt's neck.

Beatt reared back.

"I'm sorry, Beatt, I have to do it if you want to stay alive, and I have to do it now."

Mave dropped her head. She cried quietly while Turnip secured the rope into a collar around Beatt's neck.

"The Gigante are up and about," Turnip warned. "Keep your head down, stay close to me. We don't have far to go—a stall on the edge of town for the lower Gigante's horses, near the latrine—and no one will question why we're there. No one questions an idiot, so they're unlikely to question his slave."

Mave wiped her eyes then rose and took careful steps toward Beatt. "I'm steadier when I move slowly," she explained as she pulled Beatt's cape tighter about him. He stood rigidly. *I will bear this*, he thought. *If Mave can, I can.*

She patted his middle around which his tail was tightly wound. "Thank you," she said. She placed both palms over his eyes, the old gesture that symbolized the Ssha way, that darkness, the void.

He mirrored her action and placed his palms over her eyes. The three of them stood quietly for a moment. Beatt then Mave dropped their arms to their sides, Mave again pulled his cape more closely around him.

"Yes, barley cakes," called out Inna as she reentered the room. "They won't take long to fix. You stay there until I call you."

Her calloused heels scuffed the floor as she scurried to Beatt. "Goodbye," she whispered, "Thank you." She turned to the corner of the room where a shelf held bowls of barley and other grains.

Turnip opened the door and pranced on the threshold. "Time to go," he laughed and yanked on the collar.

"Mave," whispered Beatt and leaned back into the house. "I forgot to tell you. I sensed two heartbeats when I felt for you earlier and found you at the well."

Mave's face fell. "No, no, no, it can't be." She sagged against the doorframe.

"Now! Now!" called Turnip, jumping up and down. He pulled a hunched Beatt away from the house as Mave fled inside.

Beatt curved more deeply as Turnip pulled him along. It was easy to bow doubled over with grief, which assaulted him when he realized the news he had just delivered to Mave.

Chapter 4
A Disturbance Between Venus and Earth

DACE PUSHED OPEN THE CONFERENCE room door.

"...icy Dacey," she heard Josh say with a laugh as she stepped into the room.

Josh looked up with a smirk on his face. Brandon blushed.

That's me, she thought. *Whoopsie daisy, icy Dacey.* She sat down and kept her eyes on her folio screen. Time to quit fighting it or thinking it might change. She'd ask Meladee to return the shoes. She wouldn't need them.

"Mr. Dibble's all set with access," Josh said, scooping up his device as Chad did the same.

Dace said nothing as the two developers left the conference room.

"HSIN?" Brandon asked, all business.

"Homeland Security Information Network," said Dace. Her voice was flat, lifeless. "There's no 'I' between the first and second letters, but you say it as though there is."

"I know GEOV," he said, "obviously. Geographic operating

view. How about MACC?"

"Multi-agency command center. Sometimes we have to gather everyone in a central location, usually kept secret from the media and public, including people from state and federal agencies."

Brandon looked at his screen. "I think that's it," he said. "I know APIs, again, obviously, and I know what the FBI is." He tilted his head.

Dace tapped her keyboard. "I've messaged you the link to the glossary. Is that everything?"

"Yeah," he said. "Well, you know, your friend Meladee..." He stopped abruptly and flung himself back in his chair. "Wait. Thought experiment." He closed his eyes, interlaced his fingers behind his head and leaned back. "A disturbance occurs when electricity passes from Venus to Earth," he began.

Dace's fingers flew.

"The disturbance appears to be related to the difference between Venus' and Earth's size and density. How do you fix it? We don't. How do we use it? If there's activity, there's kinesis. Can't we turn that motion that into more electricity? Manually reverse the earth's poles," he finished.

He opened his eyes. "Got that?" he quizzed Dace. She nodded.

He stood. "I'm going to go find Ricci, and we'll head back to our office and get ready for the on-site testing tomorrow evening. Oh, I'll need you to come with me for a pre-test check tomorrow afternoon."

Dace sat at her desk for the next several hours and worked quietly, non-stop, as she always did, in the subterranean darkness of the office surrounded by her fellow employees in their low-walled cubes. The lulling routine allowed her to ignore the need to obtain Ricci's words she had missed until the workday was nearly done. She performed the final edits and formatting on her transcriptions so the documents were ready to upload for internal publication. She just needed to obtain the words of Ricci's she'd missed. She opened the contact info spreadsheet. She created a new contact on her phone and added Ricci's mobile number. Her body responded to having such intimate information in her phone—a thrum of pleasure pulsed through her. She messaged Meladee to say 'bye,' then messaged Ricci: "Need you to supply your comments about auras in today's meeting. Via text is fine. Thank you." Within seconds his gray reply bubbles appeared. Startled, Dace mashed her phone's power button before his transmitting message could render.

Chapter 5
Beatt Hides Then is Seen

TURNIP KEPT BEATT CLOSE TO his side as he pulled him through early-morning Apollonoulous. Beatt curled the fingers of one hand around a section of the bulge around his middle, the other yanking at the collar so he could breath. Turnip's head bobbed side to side, shaking the bells attached to his hat which rose from his head in a short cone, a miniature version of the priest's headwear during their services.

Beatt heard the voices of the few Gigante men about but, bowed low, could not look up. He wanted to; he'd never actually seen them, except through the vivid descriptions of Tear's vision when he still functioned as a half-and-half intermediary with the Ssha. He smelled them, though; sweat, horse and musk. The heady musk awakened Beatt's stem, rising under his tunic and well-wrapped cape. Turnip jerked on the collar lead, and the pinprick of pleasure faded.

When they reached the stables on the landward side of Apollonoulous, boys were bustling as they led the dozen horses out of their stalls and to the grassy pasture beyond. They glanced at Turnip then looked away; he was known everywhere in Apollonoulous and Dia for his silly, benign figure, and thus ignored.

"This is where I sleep." Turnip gestured to the end stall. Bales of hemp served as seats, and Turnip pointed to one. "Please, sit, while I get your bed ready."

Beatt sat. Light shafted through the planks of the stall. Turnip gathered the loose hemp in a corner and fluffed it up. He reached for one of his two blankets and tucked the edges of it around the oblong of hemp.

"Your couch, sire." He smiled and swept his arm out, presenting his work.

Beatt laid down. Turnip lay the other blanket on him then pulled a rectangle of fabric from his pocket.

"If you put this over your eyes, it will block the light."

Beatt's body buzzed from the overload of light beaming in through the wall's spaces. He placed the fabric over his eyes, and his muscles relaxed.

One of the boys outside shouted, and another called back. Horses' hooves stomped the ground.

"Nothing to do about the sound," said Turnip.

Without removing his eye mask, Beatt said, "How do you bear it?"

The hemp crackled as Turnip settled next to Beatt. "I do what caused the women of hieros house to punish me and give me my current name."

Old fury rose up in Beatt, and he was glad of his eye mask for surely his eyes would flare and spark at Turnip.

Maybe this is why I can't fully connect with Rowena, he thought. *I still believe only someone chosen by a woman of hieros house has the right to directly experience the Ssha way.*

Beatt was silent so Turnip would not guess his thoughts.

"As I taught myself how to dissolve into nothingness which eventually restored who I'd been, I also experienced one of the boons of becoming nothing: sensing others' thoughts and emotions. It saved me from giving myself away when in the presence of hieros house women. It also led me to others like me, self-taught in the Ssha way."

Wrath again flamed up. Beatt pressed the cloth into his brow bones. "I need time to take this in."

A wave of radiant warmth hovered over Beatt's arm then dispersed. He was glad Turnip pulled back his outstretched hand. Even a pat intended to comfort or show understanding would give the changes that had transpired a reality he clearly couldn't yet handle.

~~~

Beatt walked home in the dark of the new moon. The pitchy darkness blanketed the land in safety for prey.

The backs of his legs were tight and sore from crossing land back and forth, and his feet, even cushioned by buskins, hurt from being on them so much. His day of sinking into nothingness had allowed him to rest and restore his mind. He and Turnip shared a silent meal of steamed greens when he woke, giving his jaws respite from talking.

More to this whole process than I realized. Beatt had not needed to learn since he was very young.

Is this how this experience will change me? he thought. *Teach me humility like the women of hieros house once taught the citizens of Dia and Apollonoulous?*

I could have used a half-and-half's help, he silently railed to the Ssha deep in their crystalline caves.

Silence answered him.

Not so long ago, a half-and-half would have served as intercessor, gone out in the world as an emissary of the Ssha and even Beatt, allowing the giant reptiles with crests like tiaras on their heads and Beatt the right balance of silence, darkness and light they needed.

Now the Ssha and the half-and-halfs were safely interred, the energy they emitted slight but steady, just waiting for the boost of human connection, and there was no one to protect him from the loud, bright world.

Thudding horse hooves sounded behind him. He dropped to the ground and buried his face in his folded arms. The hooves clopped past then curved around and headed back toward Apollonoulous. Beatt lay face-down for a while. When the hooves did not return, he rose and continued his journey at a trot until the borders of Apollonoulous were well behind him.

He was accustomed to walking in the dark but not hiding as though predators might appear at any moment.

Maybe learning fear is my lesson, he thought, *so I can evade trouble as I do my part to help keep Ssha beliefs alive.*

What about Turnip? he upbraided himself. *What about Inna? Tear? Mave?*

Mave had paved the way for him and paid for it with her health. And now, as he had realized when he said goodbye to her, she would be passing a child through those brittle bones.

What will become of her? What will become of me?

He trod on the grassy plain toward the small mountain where again Nemmis would provide a day's rest. Safe under the new moon's darkness, he loosened his cape and flipped the sides over his shoulders. He untied the thin piece of cloth that secured his tail and let it unfurl then swish on the ground behind him. He loosened the ties of his long tunic that fell to his knees. The scales, a mosaic of flat plates covering his thighs and below them, but covered by his buskins, his calves, all the way down to his ankle bones, had no light to catch.

He knew how to think of the whole. Before the Gigante, that's what they—the Ssha and the people of Dia and Apollonoulous—had been.

His focal point had changed without realizing it. His

concern had shifted from the greater entity to the individuals who were a part of it, including himself.

Tear had lost his half-and-half self forever. His closest kin had, like Mave's mother, adopted the guise of a Maryannu, and, like the half-and-halfs, had accompanied the Ssha into the deepest subterranean chamber to enter the stasis. Like Tear, they had not had a choice in the matter; Ssha way, the way that powered all life from the very smallest to the very largest, dirt to the heavens, powered through them and took precedence over what they might want as individuals.

Light came upon the plain like shadow. The small mountain hunkered down in the manageable distance. Beatt's pace slowed; the sun was on its way, and the hustle and bustle of Gigante life, but he was still safe. His resting place was not far off, nor was Nemmis, not a half-and-half, not a woman of hieros house, but a friend and protector.

A rainbow of colors, orange, blue, and gray, layered the horizon as Beatt reached the small mountain. He paused at is base. The plucked remains of a season's harvest lay off to the side. Probably barley, he thought, eyeing the stalks. Troughs of water ran down the center and in ribbons a few rows from each end. The Gigante's way of keeping a water source nearby, he continued in his mind. Clever. Then he realized the Gigante would have had the people of Dia dig the canals, haul in the water, and lave the growing barley.

Beatt refastened his tail around his waist and tugged his tunic down so it covered his thighs. He climbed the path through the olive trees, now stripped of their fruit, to the top level. There he followed the path along the top ridge until he reached the cave. At its mouth he turned and faced the sun. A slice of it glowed, red and molten. Its warmth flooded over him, then, as it climbed another inch, wrapped him in its embrace. In the distance came the jostling sounds of metal against wood, horses' snorts, and guttural shouts—it was the cart coming from Dia, with its Gigante driver, the workers, and Nemmis.

Beatt's heart beat faster than usual but he attributed that to the climb.

He was close to receiving the charge he needed daily from the sun, and he lingered. A shout barked out over the plain. Beatt's outstretched arms dropped to his sides. The driver waved. He'd been seen.

Chapter 6
Descent

"MOM, IT'S ME," DACE CALLED as she let herself in the back door of her parents' house.

Mom's herb plants hung from the ceiling and occupied every available windowsill. From these pots, Mom plucked leaves to make tinctures and seasoning for her cooking. When Dace was growing up, Mom administered garlic crystallized in honey at the first sign of the flu in either Dace or Dad, but if either Dace or Mom had lingering fevers or coughs, her father whisked them off to the base Dispensary.

"In here, Dace," called Mom from deep in the house.

Dace found Mom in her reading room, where she gave tarot and I Ching readings on a small, round table draped in a black silk cloth. Mom sat at the table with three tarot on her left laid face-up in a horizontal row and three I Ching coins strewn across the table. She looked up.

"Hi, honey," she said. "How are—" she began then was overcome by a coughing fit. She sipped from a glass of water on the table. "Just a cold," Mom said between gulps. "But a bad one. Haven't had one like this since I was a kid and got bronchitis all the time."

Dace sat down in the "querent" chair, where clients sat. "Does he love me?" "Will I get the job?" most of Mom's clients asked in trembling voices. They'd never minded Dace staying in the reading room during readings, even seemed to want to draw her in to the experience, which left Dace feeling like an honorary member of a select tribe.

Mom's sandy hair was still long and hung in curtains around her face, but the muted blonde had faded to a platinum beige. Mom was shorter and lighter than Dace, and her cheekbones were high and pronounced. Her eyes tilted up at the corner. Her skin was unusually pale for someone who lived in a southeastern coastal town. To Dace she seemed to grow more diminutive and translucent with age, as though she might disappear entirely one day.

"I like your hair like that," Mom said, then gathered up the I Ching coins, shook them in her hand and dropped them onto the table. She peered at each one, noted which side was face up, and drew the sixth and final line in the hexagram. Mom looked up at Dace. "The curls that have come loose soften your face."

Dace said nothing. Everyone, even Mom, gave her advice to soften her expression. It's just my face, she wanted to say. She was used to her face, and thought she appeared neutral, which she liked. She purposely pulled her hair away from her face, to let people see who she was first. When she did let her hair down, which was rare, she looked delectable, like the foam on a latte: her sandy hair was bleached a warm gold by the sun, and her skin a light taupe. She used sunscreen, but genetics gave her naturally warm skin, not as brown as her dad's, but when combined with her mom's lighter skin, the color of coffee with cream.

"I think I'm fine to attend Jez' test descent tonight," Mom

said. "I just have this cough that's hanging on, and your dad has put his foot down about me not going. I'm sorry if he strong-armed you."

"It's okay," Dace said, leaning forward in her querent seat. "I don't mind. Really. What are you seeing in your oracles today?"

Mom frowned at the two spreads on her table. She studied the completed hexagram she'd built from six throws of the I Ching coins. "Chen, arousing shock or thunder." She shifted her gaze to the three tarot. "The Fool is in the first place or recent past position, representing someone a little naïve. The Devil in the middle represents current time and indicates someone stirring up chaos."

"Doesn't the Devil mean evil?" Dace asked.

"Not to me," Mom said. "He's just likes to cause trouble because he can."

Dace shook her head. "Doesn't sound like the oracle's for me," she said.

"Well," Mom said, peering at the layout. "The third card, the outcome, given everything else holds true, is the Hanged Man." Again, coughing erupted, and she buried her face in the crook of her elbow. As she sipped water, she looked up and saw Dace's eyes widen in concern.

"Oh, honey, no, not an actual hanging, but a change in perspective. A shift in how reality is perceived. Something big is happening, and with the three major arcana in the spread, there's no escape. I mean, it's fated. It has to happen." She regarded her daughter again. "You're sure none of this is resonating with you?"

"No, Mom," Dace said in the pleasant but flat tone Dad used to end these sorts of discussions. "Doesn't sound like you either."

"Guess not," Mom said. She sat back against the chair's

velvet cushion. "But I have to admit, I'm concerned. Hm. Well." She let her gaze drift then settle on Dace. "Dace, I really want to leave the A.R.E. and get a job at Oblation Station. It just feels right. For some reason I've never been able to advance beyond the retail shop. I don't get it. I have a degree, I've been reading oracles for others for years on my own, but they don't seem to think I have what it takes to be one of their counselors. Seems to be my lot in life. No one thinks what I experience and can demonstrate is real. I just have this feeling Oblation Station could offer me experiences beyond even what I think I want. I don't care that Oblation Station is corporate owned."

"You and Dad are an interesting mix. He's a conservative former military guy who likes rules and order, and you're his opposite in almost all ways."

"He's my rock," Mom said. She gestured to her cards and coins. "He works hard and I get to live in two worlds." She tilted her head and her eyes went soft. "I love the world that the tarot and the I Ching represent—the invisible. The only other way I would have been able to play in that world would have been to become a nun. If I get the job at Oblation Station, I'll be close to it."

"Speaking of which," Dace said. "I need to change. Be out in a few."

"Don't change too much," Mom called after her, the old family joke.

In the bathroom, Dace pulled on the white bandage skirt and short-sleeved white t-shirt. She knotted a corner of the t-shirt. She pulled out hair pins and the hair tie and let her wavy hair ripple over her shoulders and down her back.

"See you later, Mom," Dace said, leaning against the doorframe of the oracle room.

Mom looked up. Her eyes were blank. Then she registered

Dace. "Oh!" she exclaimed. "I went somewhere else for a moment."

The house was quiet with just Mom and Dace. Captain Clovis, the big gray cat, padded silently into the room and leapt up to the sunny windowsill.

"You've never told me how you came up with the name of 'Captain Clovis' for your cat," Dace said.

"Captain Clovis is his second name. My first name for him was after the being that visited me. She said her name was 'Muffalef' or something like that. Whenever I said our cat's name, it was like I was sending out a beacon to the being. 'Here I am, come to me'."

Dace laughed. "Like the bread, Muffuletta? You'd think alien beings would have more exotic names."

Mom raised her solemn face and looked at her with sad eyes. "And that's why I changed it. Everyone thought it was hilarious. I always liked 'Clovis,' the name of a prehistoric people in North America. As your Dad informed me, it's also the name of a king who established military dominance in the Roman Empire. That sealed it for your dad. Except he said we had to add 'Captain' because he couldn't have a cat outrank him. That's why he never uses just 'Clovis' like we do. No one laughed at that name. You know, my deepest wish is both you and your dad will someday believe me or at the very least stop making fun of me."

"I'm sorry." Dace rose to step next to her mother and wrap her arms around her.

"Careful, you don't want to let Dad seeing you take me seriously. That might send him right over the edge."

Dace smiled and stepped back then gathered her things. "You're pretty good at making light of what you don't like."

"Years of practice." Mom bent her head to her tarot cards and I Ching coins.

"I should go," Dace said.

"Okay," said Mom, and in an instant, though her body remained, she was gone, immersed in her own alternative world of the oracles.

Rowena paused in the doorway. Though it was a simple rectangle of wood to Dace it buzzed, as though it were a threshold between worlds, her mother's and the one most called reality.

In a burst, like a camera changing scenes, Dace's view switched, and she viewed her mother from a distance. Her mother shook her I Ching coins. Clovis rose from the sill and watched over her shoulder.

"You must sit, Clovis, when I throw the I Ching. Remember?" She twisted around to touch her nose to the cat's. He delicately sniffed her nostrils then settled his paws on her shoulder.

Her mother tumbled the coins onto to the table. She built her hexagram, consulted the *I Ching: Book of Changes*, noted the outcome, and found its written corollary in her book.

"'The taming power of the small'," she read."'The power of the shadowy.... Nine at the beginning means: Return to the way. How could there be blame in this? Good fortune....'" She kept her place in the book with one hand and with the other stroked Clovis' forehead. He rubbed his head in the crook of Rowena's neck.

"You're right, we need to see what the cards say."

She shuffled the round tarot cards by sweeping and swirling them in a loose pile on the table. Clovis nudged her with his head.

Rowena gathered the cards into a pile, cut them once to the left, then turned them up so a single card was revealed.

She showed it to Clovis who sniffed it. "Ace of Wands. Pierced by a loving force. Let's do another." She again mixed up the cards with flat hands, cut the deck and revealed a card. "Queen of Wands. A woman coming into her true self. Do you think it's me, Clovis?" The cat rolled on his side and patted her cheek. "You're right, probably not. Dace, maybe? Hold on, Clovis." She abruptly rose and Clovis dug his claws while gaining purchase with his back feet on her shoulder. He swayed as though he was riding in a litter while Rowena bent and retrieved a small box in its unopened plastic packaging.

Rowena resumed her seat at her table, and Clovis settled his hindquarters on the sill and his chest on Rowena's shoulder then folded in his paws. He perked up when Rowena took off the crackling plastic.

"In a bit," she said, patting his paws.

She loosened the neck of a cloth drawstring bag and shook out its contents. Clovis' bottom rocked as he shifted back and forth on his feet and prepared for the pounce.

From the doorway, which seemed to have turned into a time machine, Dace observed her mother slide each chip with angled shapes on it into a line.

"Never did understand how to read these," her mother murmured.

Clovis sprang, dropped onto the table, and touched a tentative paw to one of the chips. It slid easily, and Clovis cuffed it off the table. He turned to the other chips.

Rowena swept him up in her arms. "I agree, Clovis. They're only good for play. Get the plastic." She tossed the wadded ball toward the doorway. Clovis jettisoned out of her arms as though he were spring-loaded. He landed with a thump on the floor and batted the crinkly ball which hit Dace's foot.

A snap, like that of a camera shutter, and Dace's self and body were fully back in the doorway.

"Oh!" Rowena scooped the chips off the table and back into their cloth bag. "You're back. Did you forget something?"

DOWN

Clovis extricated the crumpled plastic ball from between Dace's feet and swatted it back into the room.

There are no words for this that will make sense, thought Dace, at least in the world whose rules Dace and her father observed. *I just popped in and out of time.*

Then she realized this was the moment she *could* say exactly what had happened, what had been happening as long as she could remember, including the brief encounter with Spindrift Man at the water's edge and again in the cabin bedroom so long ago.

"Don't you have a date, sweetheart?" Mom asked.

And the moment was gone.

"Right, yeah, I do. I just came back to say goodbye," she said. *Not a lie*, she reasoned. *I didn't actually say goodbye.*

"Okay, honey, bye now. Talk to you later." Mom's face blazed with her warm smile, and she blew Dace a kiss.

Dace waved and made her way to the kitchen and back door.

"Bye, honey," called Rowena as though she too existed in a world where time was so fluid with past and present she forgot she'd just said goodbye.

Dace paused in the frame of the back door. No snaps, no shifts. *Thank God.*

"Bye," she called, and her mother said something but it was too faint to hear which Dace knew meant she'd given herself back over to her world of the invisible.

Chapter 7
Heart of Beatt

BEATT LEAPT BACK INTO THE cave's shadowy entrance. The driver waved again as the cart grew ever nearer.

He turned in to the deeper darkness and, his eyes not yet adjusted, slapped his palms against the cave walls to guide himself by touch to the very back of the cave.

Surely the bones of our dead will keep the Gigante driver from coming in here, Beatt thought.

His heart thumped wildly as he hunkered down on the dirt mount. His chest hurt, and he clutched his cape to him. His breath rasped while his blood beat against his temples.

The cart creaked to a stop below him. Shouts rang out, but they were not angry; instead they were joyful. Beatt pressed himself against the back wall then dropped his face onto his folded arms. His heart banged.

"Beatt!" called out a voice from the cave entrance.

What a high voice for a Gigante, thought Beatt. He raised his head until his eyes cleared his arms.

"Beatt," sang out the voice again. "It's me, Nemmis. It's

safe. Come out."

Beatt unfolded himself from his crouch and stiff rose to his feet. He crept slowly forward, the beats of his heart slowing. But his chest still hurt, so he palmed the wall for support with one hand as he walked toward Nemmis silhouetted against the bright sun and pressed the other to his sternum.

He collapsed.

~~~

When he came to, he lay on several blankets, his cape still wrapped around him. Several faces ringed his sight. They were recognizable as citizens of Dia with their warm brown faces and short stature but also as living under Gigante rule with the men in trousers and tunics, the women in shifts and headscarves.

"Nemmis, he's awake," called one of the young women.

Nemmis knelt at his side. "I'm so sorry. We gave you a fright. I didn't mean to."

Beatt took a slow, tentative breath. The air moved easily in and out. The frantic beating of his heart had stilled, and it murmured gently in its old, slow rhythm.

"Can you sit?" Nemmis asked, and in response Beatt pushed himself up. She sat close against him, bracing him.

Beatt recoiled. Nemmis moved away.

"So sorry," she said again. "I forgot who you are for a moment. I have the cart today. Our driver, Erno, was ill, so he asked me to drive us workers to the mountain to continue mining for gold quartz. He's really an okay fellow, just big and loud."

"They're all big and loud," murmured the young woman who had hailed Nemmis.

"Do you not understand what they've done? What they've taken away from us? What they've destroyed?" Beatt thundered, his brow furrowed, and he impaled Nemmis with his furious gaze. Nemmis shrunk away and edged farther back.

Nemmis rose. "Return to the mining, everyone."

The others picked up their trowels and woven bags and set to work on both sides of the cave.

Beatt struggled to come to his feet. Nemmis stood back, and he used the cave wall for support to finally stand erect. His cape fell open. His tunic was bunched above his waist, and the scales of his tale, still wrapped securely around his waist, glistened in the sun light. Nemmis' mouth dropped open, then she snapped it shut.

"We need to get you back to Ssha Mountain where you'll be safe." She gestured toward the cave opening. "I can take you in the cart. Let's go." She turned and left the cave.

Beatt followed her down the path and into the olive trees. His feet hurt with each step, and his heart sloshed in his chest, but there was no pain.

"It's best if you're lying flat in the cart," Nemmis said when they stood at the cart.

Nemmis kept her distance as Beatt put one knee on the cart bed and heaved himself up into it. He turned himself around so his feet faced out. A glint caught his eyes. "A scale," he said, and swept it off the cart.

"No, no, no," Nemmis cried and swept down to retrieve the scale. She handed it to Beatt. "The Gigante don't have your and the hieros house women's abilities to sense conditions and other people. But they can see everything. And when they spot something that catches them they either think, 'What's this for?' or 'What can I do with this?' I don't want to risk Erno spotting anything that indicates something unusual was here."

Beatt wrapped his fingers around the scale and laid down. He held it tightly while Nemmis drove them over the plain to Ssha Mountain and said over and over to himself as the sun beat down on him, "Darkness soon, darkness soon."

DOWN

Nemmis watched from the cart parked at the foot of Ssha Mountain as Beatt wavered in front of thorny bushes.

"You're sure you've got the right place?" she asked.

He did not answer her. He was out of words. His feet burned. His blood coursed sluggishly. *Help*, he said in mind-verse to anyone who might be able to hear and assist—Mave, Anta, Audra, Mave's mother, his sister; Inna, Tear, Anta. He chanted their names in mind-verse. He added the image of the little girl, Rowena, he assumed, as he saw her for the first time as she stood on the sand, he in the water, because her name was too hard to say, even in mind-verse.

The brush blurred, and he fell forward. The thorns had melted, and he ran the several steps into the first level of the caves of Ssha Mountain.

No fire burned; only ash greeted him. He dragged himself through the first level of caves then down a steep, zig-zagging path. He sagged against the wall, rested until his breath slowed, then went down the next precipitous, back-and-forth track into the next deeper level, the last before the final sheer drop to the deepest level where the Ssha and the half-and-halfs lay in their stasis. Beatt could not enter that level; the half-and-halfs had sealed off the entrance with stacked rock. But in this third level he could rest deeply enough to enter a twilight state in which his heart would slow but not stop. He knew the risk: if he stayed in this state long enough, he would not rise again. This sounded good to him; if the Ssha required him to take over Mave's work, he would do so knowing his reward was a final rest.

He lay down in the cleft rock near a small pool of water that seeped through the cave walls from an underground spring. He imagined the pool rising and engulfing him. His heart slowed until the beats were so far apart, he dissolved himself into their nothingness.

Chapter 8
Oblation Station

DACE ARRIVED AT OBLATION STATION'S main gate. It stood open, the gate arms swept back against the chain-link fence. She drove onto the circular drive and turned off on the spoke that led to parking.

She pressed the fob to lock her Kia Soul and stared at the sky just beyond Oblation Station. Behind the boxy structure hung heavy, dense clouds, dark except for a silvery sheen in the north. The light was tinny, as though something large and metal hid behind the clouds.

The former convent was a square, beige brick building, three floors, no awnings on the windows, no porch, nothing to invite the eye to linger and instead invoking serious business, like a smaller version of the Virginia Beach Magistrate building.

Dace turned at the sound of screws clanking against metal. A woman in loose trousers and a baggy sweater pushed a sparkly blue walker along the sidewalk. She hunched over the walker as though studying the ground.

Dace walked quickly from the lot and stepped onto the sidewalk. The woman's walker rolled to a stop when she reached Dace. The woman was bent nearly in half by her curved spine. She tilted her head up to look sideways at Dace. Her smile beamed out of a face as lined as a relief map. "Can I help you, dear?"

"I'm here to sub for my mom, Rowena Banks, in some descent or something Jez Bell is putting on," Dace said.

The woman's gray head swiveled back to face her walker. "Oh!" she said, a lilt of surprise in her voice. "I didn't realize Jez had made that arrangement. Guess I missed the memo."

Dace smiled. "Well, she didn't, actually. My dad did." Dace paused when Agnes was silent. "My dad, Connor Banks? Local businessman? Member of Ruritan Club that helps out the community?"

"Ah," Agnes said, nodding. "I know the Ruritan Club. We'll see what Abby says. She's a Descender and helps Jez with descents. I'll take you where you need to go."

She revolved in a slow circle, picking up and setting down the walker with each step, until she faced the opposite direction.

"This way, dear," she said as Dace followed her up a ramp into the center's front door. "I'm Agnes, by the way."

"Nice to meet you Agnes By-the-Way," Dace said, and Agnes laughed, looking back at her in her sideways fashion. "I'm Dace."

"It's a pleasure to meet you," Agnes said. "And perhaps host you, if Abby agrees to the subbing arrangement."

"You're one of the oblates?" Dace asked as she walked with Agnes toward a ramp alongside the building.

"You might say the head oblate." Agnes lifted her walker over the lip of cement between the sidewalk and the ramp, setting it down with a little thump.

"Oh!" It was Dace's turn to be surprised. Agnes emanated friendliness, warmth, and accessibility. Dace would have expected the head oblate to be distant though kind and cutting an imposing figure, in a habit with voluminous black sleeves that spread like angel's wings when she held her arms out.

Dace walked alongside Agnes as she rolled her walker up the ramp, her breathing becoming more audible with each push. She paused outside the main door, and Dace pushed the large, rectangular button. While the door wheezed open, Agnes' labored breathing calmed. She pushed her walker inside and Dace followed.

In the circular reception area, a beam of sunshine shone down from a round skylight in the domed ceiling. A front desk sat empty. The center gift store behind the front desk was also empty, closed and dark. "We have encouragers!" read a placard in the store's display window. "Rings, bracelets, and charms to protect you from harm and attract abundance!" "Spiritual and physical wellness found here!"

Agnes rolled a few feet down a hall off the circular lobby and halted outside a room. She gestured to the room. "Abby will be with you in a minute. You can wait in here." She bestowed another smile as bright as a blessing on Dace, then tottered away gripping the handles of her glittering walker.

Dace waited in the room, furnished with a cot, a desk, and a lamp that cast a solitary spot of yellow light. A small window faced north. On the wall hung three plaques: "For those times when you aren't where you used to be but aren't yet where you're going," read one. It was signed by Jez in large, curvy letters with print underneath so tiny Dace had to peer at it from inches away: "from Sylvia Brinton Perera's *Descent to the Goddess*." The second plaque had the heading, "Oblation Station's motto," with text running underneath:

"We must be still and still move into another intensity." The third plaque read:

Come, come, whoever you are.
Wonderer, worshipper, lover of leaving.
It doesn't matter.
Ours is not a caravan of despair.
Come, even if you have broken your vow
a thousand times
Come, yet again, come, come.

Red scrawls on the other wall caught her eye but then a woman in a dun-colored shift and headscarf came into the room. Her face was as broad as a baby doll's, wide, planed bones, her eyes large and long lashed.

"Hello," she said, extending her hand, "I'm Abby." She took Dace's hand, held it briefly, then released it from her gentle grip. "You're inquiring about our descents?"

Dace shook her head. "No, I'm here to stand in for my mother, Rowena Banks, in a test descent Jez asked her to participate in. My mom is sick and can't come tonight."

Abby frowned. "Descenders usually require some preparation, even for test descents."

"I have to do this, please," Dace said. She couldn't let her father down after she'd given her word. "I just have to. Please let me."

Abby's face filled with light. "You have the passion!" she exclaimed. She clasped her hands in front of her heart.

She grabbed Dace's wrists and brought her radiating face close. Dace leaned back.

"I, too, have the fire," Abby said. "I recognize it in you as clearly as I saw it in myself."

She released Dace's wrists. "We'll take it as providence

that your mother could not descend tonight and that you, someone who is clearly called to the void and other worlds, must go in her place."

"What about Jez?" Dace rubbed her wrists and took another step back should Abby's passion erupt again.

"Jez will be fine with this," she assured Dace. "She understands the fire that can only be quenched by a dive into the void."

Oh, good Lord, thought Dace. *At least I hope you are*, she finished in her thoughts, remembering Oblation Station's former identity.

"This is just a test descent, but even so the rule is you must observe silence during the retreat," Abby said, nearly chirping with delight at her new-found soul friend. "Once you've entered the descent area, you must not utter a sound." She paused. "It's the silence that does it. That's what moves you into other realms."

"Am I likely to run into other descenders?" Dace asked.

Abby shook her head. "Not yet. But there will be more. And soon." Abby smiled. She looked out the window and stepped near it, gesturing for Dace to join her. Dace took a tentative step forward but kept her distance. "The light behind the clouds," Abby continued. "Do you see it?"

Dace saw it; it was the same, strange, metallic light she'd seen when she got out of the car. "You mean the setting sun?" she asked in the same neutral tone she used with her mother when she became fervent about a metaphysical concept.

Abby shook her head. "The light changed about a year ago. I saw it. It was as though someone turned the lights up. You don't understand, not yet, but you will. The veil between the worlds is thinning. Jez is one of the first to live-cross worlds, navigate the rules of our world and that world. You have no idea how huge this is." She glanced at the desk and up at the wall with the red scrawls. She smiled. "Look." She picked up the goose-neck lamp and held its light to the writing that looped along the wall.

"Jez is communicating with us as she moves behind the veil," Abby said, setting the lamp down. Dace strained to read the dim writing. "Jez is in the Void. The Void is where we all start from, where we all end up. She's in the place we all want to be. Where you might be when you descend."

A clock struck the hour. Five bells tolled for the late September afternoon.

"It's time," Abby said. "Follow me."

They passed Agnes as they went down the hall. Agnes nodded at Abby and tilted her head to smile at Dace. Dace turned to watch Agnes' retreating back, draped in a cardigan and bent to the curving shape of the earth.

Abby opened a door. "You go down to the basement," she said. "It will be clear what to do when you get to the bottom of the steps."

Glad of her sturdy Oxfords, Dace tentatively touched one foot down, then another. Her rubberized soles made a squelching sound.

Abby shut the door behind her, sending her into darkness. Dace stumbled and grabbed the stair rail. "Great, Jez," she muttered, "You've got both trip hazards and lack of accessibility." She waited on the stair until her eyes adjusted to the gloom and continued cautiously down.

At the bottom, a glow beckoned from the passageway. Dace cautiously turned the corner into a hallway. Sconces with dim lights ran the length of it. The wind had picked up, and it howled beyond the cinder block walls.

The feather brushed her neck in a long stroke from the soft fringe to the calamus scraping across the tiny hairs at her nape.

The moist basement air enveloped Dace like a cloud of live things. Blindly, she reached out for something to grab but there was nothing there except the sconces placed high on the wall and the cold block walls which were probably made of cement and ashes. She pressed her palms against the walls, the chill reminding her where she was in space. Lat, long, lat, long, she repeated to herself to calm the frenzied feeling rising in her. *This is for Mom, this is for Dad*, she continued in her thoughts. True words, but they didn't calm her wild fear. Straighten up and fly right, she admonished herself. She slapped the back of her neck. The ghostly plume ceased its chilling caress. Her fear calmed sufficiently, allowing her to push off the wall and continue.

She paused at the first station, an alcove lit by a soft light. A note instructed her to hang her worldly belongings on the hook provided. She hung her bag then paused; did nuns steal? *Former nuns*, she reminded herself. *But do oblates steal?* her thoughts continued. *Could the whole thing be a racket, a set up to plunder unwary pilgrims? Stop it*, she said sternly to herself, and proceeded farther into the passageway.

She imagined she was her dad's wingman on a new mission, flying into unknown territory. He'd told her of those times when he'd had to rely on his training and his confidence in his skills to quell racing thoughts anticipating what might happen.

What little light was available faded as Dace advanced in the corridor. A buzzing ensued as she imagined the invisible presences came back into full power. "No," she whispered, "I will not let you scare me. In fact, I won't let you exist. You aren't real."

She slid her hands along the stony walls, beckoned by a faint light.

She arrived at the second station. A light illuminated

another note. It read, "Now hang yourself upside down and experience the power of the goddess." A wide swath of fabric hung in front of her. She tugged it. It was stretchy. She released it, and it bounced. Her eyes traveled the band's length to the ceiling where the continuous loop traveled over the top of a strong wooden beam. She pulled at both sides of the material, and found it was double-fold, like a kind of hammock.

"Oh, for God's sake, Jez," Dace said aloud. "You've designed something only a chosen, able-bodied few can get into." How could Jez have imagined her mother would be able to do this? Mom's arthritis wasn't severe but it was everywhere in her body.

Disgusted by these thoughts of Jez, Dace's tremors of fear faded. Imagining the scathing review she could post on social media, she hiked her bandage skirt around her hips, rose to her toes, and hefted her bottom into the swing. She scooched forward until her feet reached the block walls. She frog-walked up the wall until she hung upside down as though encased in a stork's bundle. The edge of the band settled neatly into her hip joints, and held her securely.

"Utterly ridiculous," Dace muttered once her back rested against the wall, encased in her upside-down hammock. Who could manage such a setup? Certainly not her mother. She was healthy but with her joints stiff from arthritis and the discs in her spine were ground down from early degeneration. she would have trouble hoisting herself into the descent contraption. In fact, it was the one yoga trend her mother would not even try, which made Dace and her father happy.

The knotted ropes creaked as Dace settled in. Her simmering indignation quieted as she hung, bat-like, her eyes clouding as the blood rushed to her head. The bands provided traction for her spine and her body weight gently stretched the ball joints in her hips away from the sockets. She lowered her arms and touched her fingertips to the floor, then folded her arms below her head. All the bones in her body seemed to come apart, like pieces of a space station moving away from each other in the vacuum of outer space. Her bones resolved to their natural state, matter with great gaps of space between them. Her mind followed suit. Her brain waves dropped from the chatter of beta into theta then the edges of gamma. Her consciousness left the confines of her body.

When her eyes opened, she stood in a softly lit cubby with three others, two women and a man. The two women huddled against each other, and the fellow turned in a slow circle in his t-shirt and drawstring pants. His mouth hung open in bewilderment as he took in Dace then continued his tiny circle until he again faced front. Dace pressed past her cubby-mates and stood at the edge of their compartment.

They were in a ship's cavernous hold. It was lined on both sides with about one hundred people gathered in groups of three or four in their respective recessed spaces in the wall. Some of the people, like Dace, were dressed in everyday clothing, but others were dressed in what looked like sleepwear—loose tops and shorts or drawstring pants. A few were in their underwear. All appeared baffled and slightly stunned, looking around with startled and confused expressions. Dim green lights inset in the walkway shone like a divers' flashlight through sea water. At the front, a dais sat empty, illuminated by a soft spotlight.

Dace was tickled; in all her strange, secret experiences she'd had since she was a child, she'd never had partners. As an only child in waking life, she'd stored up a lifetime of thoughts about what it would be like to have siblings. This was the next best thing: cohorts in an other-worldly encounter.

Markings on one of the metal walls of her space caught her eye. They looked like shorthand, the symbols with their curvy swoops and loops used by stenographers. A short message was at Dace's eye level, which meant the typical viewer was no taller than she, barely topping five feet. Perhaps the message was in all the shallow cubbies? she wondered. "Remain calm, all shall be revealed," she imagined, and smiled to herself. Or perhaps it was cleaning instructions for the ship's maintenance crew: "Disinfect after mass abductions."

A rustling sounded at the front of the hold. Everyone turned toward it. Dace peered between cubby mates to see.

Three women stood on the dais, each wearing a jewel-toned gown: ruby, sapphire, and topaz. The woman in ruby turned like a door opening, and a dark-haired man wearing a dun-colored shift materialized out of the darkness. His shoulders were broad and his long hair was tied at the nape of his neck. His gaze swept up and down each. His eyes lighted on Dace. A look of relief washed over his face. He stepped down from the dais and strode the length of the aisle toward Dace, his tail of bound hair swinging back and forth.

When he reached Dace's compartment, her cubby mates shrank back, exposing Dace. The man extended his arms to her as though greeting a long-lost friend. His dark pupils were diamond-shaped, like that of a snake.

Dace's brain sprang into alert: friend or foe? Stay or flee?

Dace blinked, and she was back in Oblation Station's basement, hanging upside down in the wall hammock.

She grasped the rubbery edges and hauled herself up. She rocked herself out of the cloth until her feet touched down on the concrete floor.

She stumbled back the way she'd come, tripping over her feet. She retrieved her bag; she squeezed it to confirm a wallet-like bulk, then staggered up the stairs. At the top she pounded frantically on the door.

Abby swung it open, a broad, knowing smile on her face. Agnes stood next to her, her head in its forced bow. She teetered a step forward, gripping the handles of her walker, and placed her warm palm on Dacey's forearm.

Unexpected tears ran down Dace's cheeks.

With a gentle pat to Dace's arm, Agnes angled away and departed down the hall.

Dace's tears continued to flow. Abby looked discreetly away.

"A little rest might be a good idea before you re-enter the outer world," Abby said. "Come with me." Abby turned, but Dace remained where she was, overcome. Abby shifted course, came back and slipped her arm through Dace's and led her down another hall lined along both sides with doors and plaques that read "retreatant."

"Here," she said, opening one of the doors and gesturing for Dace to enter.

Dace stepped in and surveyed the room. It was small and cell-like, furnished with a cot, a bedside table, and a sink. A window looked out on Oblation Station's backyard, a view on the dusk turning to night. The pink azaleas peppered with brown petals were an impressionistic blur though her veil of tears.

Dace slowly lowered herself to sit on the cot, and Abby slipped quietly out and closed the door softly behind her.

A plinking tune came from her bag. Dace turned her head toward the bag. The sound's meaning eluded her. Another tune came a few minutes later, one she vaguely recognized, but even so Dace's gaze remained on the azaleas.

She remained there as the waxing moon became visible, low in the sky. She lay down on her cot and fell asleep.

When she woke a few hours later, a presence with glowing

orbs for eyes was in the room, beside her bed. It was breathing. Panicked, Dace's heart raced and her breath came in short, shallow gasps. She tried to rise but something held her down. She willed herself to fight it, but she'd become paralyzed. She lay there, heart pounding, terror ricocheting through her mind.

Scream, she said to herself, *scream.*

Wispy breath hovered near her ear. The outline of a face gradually materialized inches above hers. It was flattened and leonine but contoured, as though it were a mask moving from two dimensions into three.

A being materialized. With a head of long, dark hair gathered at the nape of his neck, he was broad, heavy-limbed, wearing a dun-colored shift. He had a nose like a snake's snout. His orbs dimmed and redefined themselves into eyes. In the light of the moon, his diamond-shape pupils shone. His eyes grew bright, even merry. It was the man from the ship's hold.

As he gazed into Dace's eyes, Jack Ricci's face appeared as a transparent overlay. Dace gasped. The paralysis faded. She felt the full length and weight of Ricci's body. She arched against him, and he responded, pressing himself into her. Ricci's eyes softened, and Dace's lids closed in sleepy pleasure. Then the weight of him began to lighten. Dace's eyes flew open. She pushed her body into the dissolving Ricci, melting into his half-materialized form. Her eyes locked with his and, panicked, they tried to hold on to each other. Then there was only his transparent face receding and that, too, faded away, leaving the face of the snake-eyed man. He, like Ricci, began to dissolve, and he held Dace's gaze as long as he could before he too faded to nothing.

Desolate, Dace fell back asleep. In her dreams, her snake-eyed man played an instrument like a didgeridoo and shot tiny, white feathers into the air.

She woke in the gray dawn, forcing her eyes open. She rolled onto her side and slowly took in what greeted her: tiny, white feathers littering the floor.

She stumbled out of bed and began scooping up the feathers and tossing them out of the window. Obviously, like so many events in her life, this type of thing must not be talked about. If Jez knew of this, she'd announce it to the world as proof of the power of her descents, miracles like Mary's face appearing in a pan of scrambled eggs: evidence of the divine veils lifting. With each toss, a curl of wind hijacked the feathers, and they rode back into the room. Finally, Dace balled them up and dropped the matted mess with a plunk into the bushes outside her window.

Her heart and limbs heavy, Dace dressed and gathered her things.

"Good morning, Dace Banks!" called a voice from behind the reception desk as Dace floated like a ghost through the lobby.

Dace paused and turned. "I'm Elizabeth," said the heavy-set woman with a halo of white, fluffy hair. "One of the oblates. Please join us for breakfast. Plenty of oatmeal and brown sugar to offer!"

Still mute, Dace shook her head, waved wanly and continued her way to the door.

She stepped off the sidewalk onto the gravel parking lot surface, and a wave of longing to return to the center rolled over her. Lat, long, lat, long, she repeated to herself. She took a few more steps. Another wave hit. She missed Agnes's gentle kindness and care, the simple, bare retreatant room and the welcoming energy of Elizabeth. More than anything she missed that strange, dream-like moment with Ricci. She wobbled on the uneven gravel and stopped in the middle of the lot.

A white Tahoe backed out of a space at the lot's end and started forward toward the exit to the circular drive. The car slowed then stopped as it came abreast of Dace. The window descended.

"Dace? Dace Banks?"

A face loomed out of the open car window. It was Jack Ricci.

Dace stared at him. She couldn't speak. Tears welled in the back of her throat. She swayed as she grew light-headed.

"Hold on," Ricci said. "Stay there. Don't move."

He reversed, swung the car back into its space, and parked. He jumped out of the Tahoe and ran to Dace's side. He wore a dark suit, like yesterday, except this one was a rich black with subtle stripes paired with a white shirt. His tie was a soothing navy and sky blue with a red dot in the middle. As she stared at the red dot, the spinning in her head calmed.

"Are you all right?" Ricci asked.

Her voice wavery from held-back tears, she said, "I went on one of Jez Bell's test descents, taking my mom's place, and it wrecked me." She crossed her arms and ferociously rubbed her upper arms. "It's so cold out here."

Ricci slipped out of his suit jacket and draped it around her shoulders.

Encased in Ricci's warmth and scent, Dace's shoulders sagged and tears again welled in her eyes.

Ricci pulled a folded white handkerchief from his trouser pocket. "Here," he said. His eyes shone with warmth and concern behind his wire-rim spectacles. He dabbed the tears running down her cheeks then pressed the handkerchief into her hand.

Dace's tears poured out, and then Ricci's arms were around her, pulling her tightly to him. She buried her face in his shoulder and sobbed.

When the crying slowed, her tense neck and shoulder muscles relaxed. Ricci's feet were planted apart, Dace's in between them. He felt good. She shifted in his hold, fitting herself more comfortably against him. His body was broad--protective--and muscular and very, very warm. He shifted slightly to fit himself more comfortably against her. She lifted her forehead off his shoulder and met his eyes. They were soft and heavy-lidded, as they'd been in her dream vision last night. Lost in their liquid darkness, Dace pressed her body against his and his hard-on. Ricci jumped back.

Dace buried her face in her hands. "I'm so sorry," she wailed, handing him his suit jacket. "I could be fired for that. I don't know what's happening to me. I'm so totally sorry. Report me to Mr. Dad—I mean my Banks. Oh fuck. I mean Mr. Banks. I have to go." With her head bowed as deeply as Agnes', she ran to her car. Ignoring Ricci in her peripheral vision, she floored the gas. A wash of gravel spat up behind her tires as she tore out of the lot.

Once out of the Oblation Station gate, she drove around the block then pulled over. Her heart raced. Lat, long, lat, long, she repeated to herself, and the familiar drill calmed her. She watched in her rearview mirror until Ricci's white Tahoe passed by on the cross street. Her breathing slowed, and with it her heartbeat. She gave her head a little shake and put her blinker on to pull out into the street. Only then did it occur to her to ask herself: What was Jack Ricci doing at Oblation Station?

Chapter 9
The Uses of Frost

BACK AT HER STUDIO APARTMENT, Dace showered. She brewed coffee, drank a cup, then ate a strawberry Pop-Tart. Her second cup of coffee in hand, she studied the contents of her closet and clothes drawer. She put on her secret weapon underwear: a black plunge bra, black lacy thong panties, and a garter that held up silky, thigh-high stockings. She pulled on a gray knit pencil skirt, midi-length, and a collared, long-sleeved white shirt that she buttoned to the top. She applied her usual makeup: mascara, a dot of highlighter in the corner of her eyes to mask the ever-present darkness, and raspberry sheer lipstick. She twisted her long, wavy hair, nappy from the humidity, into a top knot. For the finishing touch, she inserted pearl stud earrings in her ears.

Finally, she checked her phone for messages. Anxiety and anticipation mounted as she scrolled down to Ricci's. "Here you go: 'Auras are what lay people call this electromagnetic field. But you don't need mystical powers to measure them. Just the right technology, including a very strong signal, and

Brandon's—Mr. Dibley's—app and the APIs.' Let me know if you need anything else."

Her heart thudded. She imagined a frost encasing it, and the beats slowed.

Her composure regained, she skimmed her other messages. Dad had sent the list of volunteers for tomorrow's testing. Only Meladee's name appeared on the list. The three required attendees were Josh, Chad, and Dace. If they couldn't get at least two more, they'd have to cancel.

Dace slipped on and tied her black Oxford lace-ups. On the way out the door, she grabbed another foil packet of Pop-Tarts and her aviator-style sunglasses that she'd purchased long ago to match those her dad favored ever since his days as a Navy fighter pilot.

At work, she powered up her desktop machine then bent to flip the toggle switch for the under-cabinet fluorescent lights hidden behind glass plates. The harsh light shone on her desk and revealed the dust-free surface her dad insisted on.

"Bad girl," Meladee stood at her cube and whispered.

Dace turned. "Oh, Meladee, you don't know the half of it." Tears welled once again in her eyes.

Meladee's brow furrowed in concern. She came around the wall into Dace's cube. "What happened?" she asked softly.

Dace shook her head. "You won't believe it."

"Miss Gomez, Miss Banks, good morning."

Dace's father stood as straight as a ramrod outside her cube. He wore his military-issue khaki trousers, a white dress shirt, and tie.

Meladee jumped. "Hi, Mr. Banks. Miss Banks, see you later," she said and sped off to her cube.

Dace stood with a straight spine, shoulders back, as though at attention. "Mr. Banks, I request five minutes with you, sir," she said.

"Granted," Dad said. "But no more than that. Scrum starts in ten."

Dace followed him to his office, the only one with a door. Dad sat down behind his desk and Dace sat down in what the employees called the hot seat.

Dace knew what she had to say—tell Dad the truth of what had happened with Ricci in the Oblation Station parking lot, then resign—but the words would not come out of her mouth.

"Miss Banks," her father said. He rose to close the door and came back to his chair. "Dace," he said. "This has to be quick. If I don't tolerate lateness in employees, I can't tolerate it in myself. Or you."

"I know," Dace said, letting out a breath she didn't know she was holding. Lat, long, lat, long, she repeated to herself.

At that moment, her father's phone pinged. He glanced at it. "I have to take this," he said. "It's Jack Ricci."

Dace's heart sank.

Dad remained silent, listening to Ricci.

"I see," Dad said after a few minutes. He looked at Dace.

Damn it, she thought. Ricci had gotten to the noble action first. Crap.

Dad swiveled in his chair to face the window. "I trust our additional terms remain in place?" he asked then paused as he listened. "Excellent. Thank you."

Dad tapped the phone and put it on the desk. "Mr. Ricci is no longer with us," he said. "A personal matter."

Dace stared at her father. "That's all he said?"

"Actually, he said, 'a very pressing personal matter,' but he didn't offer any details."

Dad rose, gathering up his Notebook and phone for the scrum. "Mr. Dibble is still here, though, and you will need to stay extra close to him starting right now and scribe everything he says, whether it makes sense or not, any time, day or night. We won't have Mr. Ricci as a second pair of official ears. We can get another engineer to evaluate Brandon's final ideas." Both Dad's devices pinged. "Scrum's starting in five," he said and strode out of his office.

Dace slumped in the chair. Ricci had saved her.

"Miss Banks," her father barked from the doorway.

Dace jumped up and joined her father.

The developers and Brandon huddled like a football team before a play. Dace stood at the edge of their huddle with her folio sitting on a ledge at waist level, her hands poised over the keyboard.

"Sir," began Chad, and she captured what he had accomplished the day before, what he would accomplish today, and any roadblocks he was currently encountering. He ended with a final, "Sir," and Josh took the handoff. "Sir," he began and reported in the same fashion. Without prompting, and as though he'd practiced, Brandon began, "Sir," described his thought experiment of the day before and ended with "sir."

After the scrum, Dace left quickly and sped to Meladee's cube. "Meladee," she panted, out of breath, as she skidded to a halt at her desk.

"Oh my God, come on, let's get coffee," Meladee hissed, jumping up and snatching her bag.

"Miss Banks," Brandon rasped in a hushed voice, his long legs scissoring toward her. "Thought experiment."

Dace mouthed, "Help!" at Meladee, her eyes wide and pleading.

"Hey, there, mister new guy." Meladee jumped out into the aisle.

Heads popped up from their cubes like gophers out of their prairie holes. Meladee wasn't using her inside voice.

A bloom flooded up Brandon's neck and into his face as he furiously blushed. He opened and closed his mouth but no words came out. He made an about-face "Changed my mind," he called. "My cube."

As They Who Ride employees looked on in disbelief at yet another person not using their inside voice, Brandon charged away.

Meladee flew back to her cube and dumped the contents of her bag under the shelf lights. Quietly she uncapped an amber prescription bottle and tapped out two white, oval pills. She wrapped them in a tissue and tucked them into Dace's bag. "They're antihistamines with a boost: they quiet your brain. Hydroxyzine. Take in case of mental emergency."

"Thank you," Dace whispered with tears in her eyes, blurring the sight of her confounded coworkers.

She ran to catch up with Brandon. As she neared him, he braked to a halt, and Dace smacked into him. He didn't notice. "I have a different idea," he said. "Let's go to the scenario testing site. I can dictate the thought experiment as we go."

Brandon strode out of the office and to the elevator with Dace at his side. He rambled about the earth's electromagnetic poles changing with regularity, and she tilted her folio up and toward him so that the voice-activated software captured his speaking. When he unlocked the passenger side of his black SUV, she hoisted herself in and leaned out of the car door as he went around to the driver's side so she could transcribe in old-fashioned shorthand what he was saying. He was still talking as he got in, started the car, and pulled out of the lot and onto Arrowhead Road. As he drove, Dace bent her head to her folio and resumed inputting his words by typing on her keyboard. His stream of words was relentless, fast, hard and non-stop like a firehose of water. She did not raise her head as he turned a corner, slowed, pulled in, then stopped the engine.

We're here, Dace typed.

"We're here," Brandon said.

Dace looked up. They had arrived at Oblation Station. She rubbed her forehead. *What. The. Fuck*, she thought.

Brandon opened his door and swung his legs out. "My sister gets us a discount on renting the retreat center's basement rooms for our scenario testing."

Dace scrambled out of the car and ran to catch up with Brandon who was halfway up the handicapped ramp.

"Your sister?" she asked, out of breath.

"Yeah," he said, "Jez. Jez Bell. Maybe you've heard of her? She's got some alternative spirituality thing going." He flung open the door and strode inside the lobby.

Dace stopped. Her jaw hung slightly open. The door wheezed as it closed slowly on its pneumatic hinge.

The door opened again and Brandon stuck his head out. "Coming?"

Dace jumped and followed him inside, her mind racing.

"Hey Obi-Wan Elizabeth," Brandon called to the woman who had greeted Dace that morning.

Elizabeth erupted in giggles. "Oh, you, Brandon," she said. "Your usual room in the basement is all ready for you."

Dace's head swam with memories of the night before as she followed Brandon to the elevator. Instead of B he pressed S. The car went one floor below the basement, and the door swooshed open. Dace followed Brandon into the subbasement. Like the descent area, the halls were lit by electric wall sconces.

Brandon opened a door and flipped on the lights. Dace stepped into the room. Several bare bulbs hung on cords from beams lining the unfinished ceiling. The floor was concrete. Brandon placed his feet apart and waved his hands up and down in slow motion. Then he twisted rapidly back and forth, the momentum flinging his arms to either side.

He brought his feet back together and marched. "Just warming up," he said. "Hand me your phone. I need to install the GEOV app."

She handed him her phone, and both were silent as he peered at it and tapped.

"Almost there," he said. "Okay, you're set. You need to keep Locations on for it to work properly."

"Brandon, I have to ask you," Dace said as she dropped her phone into her bag. "My dad, sorry, I mean Mr. Banks, he hired you even though you're Jez Bell's brother?"

"Because I'm Jez Bell's brother. Or at least that's what I assume. I mentioned Jez was my sister and that she helped us arrange the room rental here at the Station, and Mr. Banks mentioned your mom is trying to get a job here. Mr. Banks helps us, my sister helps your mom. Quid quo pro. You'll have to ask Jack. He took care of those contractual details. I'm just the idea guy. And on that note, I'm getting something." He paced the length of concrete room floor, back and forth from end to end. "What if we could shift the poles ourselves?"

Her hands shook as they hovered above the keyboard to input Brandon's words. Inside Dace, her world was falling apart. All her mental constructs that created the constants in her life broke apart and tumbled like sticks. Her father had hired Brandon and Ricci as a favor for a favor? This was strictly against the professional ethics he professed, and definitely against government contract requirements. Lat, long, lat, long, she said to herself. *Damn lat and long!* she screamed in her mind. She slammed her folio shut.

She ran out of the room, and the elevator doors closed on Brandon's faint voice continuing his thought experiment. Through her tears, she blindly pressed buttons. The door opened on a hall identical to the first level. She ran to the left and instead of the lobby encountered another hall, but one with an open door and light spilling out of it. For a moment she thought she had entered a different reality then noticed the high branches of a magnolia tree outside the window at the end of the hall. She realized she was on the wrong floor. A voice murmured from the room with the open door. Dace stepped quietly toward it.

"Peter, your role is to alert the descenders. I'll text you when it's time to call my brother and ask if he's seen me. By then he'll have done everything I expect him to when I don't answer his calls or texts for several hours. He'll call the police then he'll go over to my condo. He'll see the writing on the wall. Ha! Yeah, true, a fact and a cliché. I'll leave a clue that will bring him from my place here to Oblation Station where I'll just be returning from a descent to the void." A woman paused in her talking. "Believe me, I know my brother. He'll behave exactly like I predict."

Dace crept closer and cautiously peered into the room. A woman sat with her back to the door and her phone pressed to her ear. A bounty of dark, thick, luxurious hair tumbled down her back. She wore a dun-colored shift, and a matching head scarf lay on the desk next to her.

"You get the descenders here en masse, and we'll get enough media coverage for the descents to really take off."

It was Jez Bell.

"No, weirdly, Agnes doesn't mind. She seems to understand the importance of the bottom line." Jez laughed at something Peter said. "Definitely! Gotta keep the revenue coming in," she said. "Okay, let's go over the plan one more time."

Dace stepped quietly back down the hall to the elevator. Her eyes were dry now. Her jaw was set in fury.

She flew out of Oblation Station. She stared at Brandon's black SUV. *Damn*, she thought. She used her phone to hail a ride share and waited for the car outside the Station gates.

Mister fly right, she thought. *Mister tight ship*. She'd restrict him to base, alright. She imagined his face when he realized she could turn him in, land him in prison, that she had that kind of power.

Her phone chimed as the driver neared the office. The display read *Mom*.

Oh, God. Mom, thought Dace. *What will this do to her?*

"I changed my mind," Dace said to the driver. "Change of destination address." The driver pulled over to input Dace's home address. Dace texted her dad: Not feeling well. Heading home for the day.

Within a few minutes, Dace stood in the calm of her apartment. She unmuted her phone's ringer. It jangled with Meladee's fractured ring, a riff from The Residents' "Constantinople." Dace let it play until the call went to voicemail. Then she texted Meladee: Just not feeling great. Talk to you later. Then she texted Brandon: sorry, coming down with something. Out for the day.

Who's your sub? Brandon texted her back.

Ask Mr. Banks, she responded.

Okay. Later.

Her phone pinged with a message from Ricci: Can I see you?

Dace squashed her thumb against the power button and let the screen go dark. The possibility of Ricci entering her life included the possibility of him exiting, and it was all too much to contemplate.

She rummaged in her bag for the two Hydroxyzine Meladee had given her earlier. She lay them on a cutting board in her tiny kitchen. She cut one in half with a paring knife and reduced it to crumbs. She sliced through the remaining pill with a quick chop of a chef's knife and placed the cleanly-cut half-pill on her tongue and washed it down with a swig of water from a bottle on the table in front of her couch. She stared out at the silver maple outside her window. The light green leaves with their silvery underbellies shook in the September wind. Her mind was ablaze: How could her dad have done this, what a hypocrite, how could Brandon and Ricci have done this, why did Ricci have to comfort her just before she found out he was in cahoots with her father and Jez?

Dace bolted forward. She remembered Brandon saying Ricci had been married to his sister. The realization fully hit Dace: Ricci had been married to Jez.

It wasn't long before the half a Hydroxyzine took effect. The jabbing phrases calmed down. Her eyelids drooped. She swiveled around on the couch and lay her head on the pillow. Soon she was asleep.

When she woke, the apartment was gloomy, everything shrouded in shades of black and grey in the falling dusk. She picked up her phone. Three voicemails from Ricci. They were identical: "Dace, it's Jack Ricci. Please call me." His voice was even and cool. She detected only reason, no emotion. Apparently he'd moved beyond their brief moment this morning, and she'd misunderstood his reason for wanting to see her. *I can do that too*, Dace thought. *I know how to be ice. All right, Jack Ricci, time to learn how I earned the nickname, "Icy."*

She pressed Call Back.

"Dace," Ricci answered in his even voice.

"Yes," she said. Her memory and emotions of that morning sealed over like the surface of a pond turning to frosty crystals.

"Can I see you?"

She began to relax as her emotions safely froze over. "All right. Where?"

"Do you know where the Bahama Breeze is?"

Ironic, thought Dace. "I do," she said.

"Very good," he said. "Seven o'clock?"

"Yes," she said and ended the call.

Chapter 10
Manifestation

SHE WAITED NEAR THE MAÎTRE d's stand at Bahama Breeze. At home, she'd taken off her secret weapon underwear and put on her ugliest of panties, beige boy shorts with tight elastic, and a sports bra, designed to mash her breasts. Her dirndl hung to her ankles and one of her dad's white undershirts billowed above it. She wore her black Oxfords with no socks. Her hair was pulled back tight with no pretty curls escaping. She'd taken off the day's makeup and had not replaced it, so her light eyebrows blended into her latte skin, her naturally peach lips the only hint of color.

When Ricci entered the restaurant, his eyes found her immediately.

"Dace," he said, coming to stand in front of her. "I'm glad you could make it. How are you feeling after this morning?"

"After the most embarrassing moment of my life?" she asked.

"I guess that answers the question," he said.

His look of hurt and disappointment surprised Dace, and

she leaned forward. Then she caught herself and stepped back. "Maybe this wasn't such a good idea."

"Dace—" Ricci stepped closer to her and took her hand. He held it lightly in his warm palm, and she was acutely aware of his thumb on her knuckles and the heaviness in her pelvis.

A wave of emotion broke over her and she closed her eyes. She snatched her hand back and opened her eyes. "We cannot be doing this," she said, "It's against company policy. No intimate relationships with coworkers, clients, or business partners."

"I'm not any of those now." Ricci took her hands in his, as though about to take vows.

"Ricci," called the maître d'. "Party of two."

Ricci turned away briefly to speak to the maître d'. The insulating layer of warmth around Dace cooled. He turned back to Dace. She pulled him toward her. The lapels of his jacket brushed against her chest. His warm exhales brushed her lips.

She abruptly stepped back. "Thirty minutes," she said, smoothing her dirndl skirt.

Ricci lightly touched Dace's mid-back they followed the maître d' to their table situated in the center of the restaurant.

Dacey sat down and glanced at their table's clear path to the door.

"In case you need to flee," Ricci said.

Dace smiled. "I guess I have that habit."

After they had ordered drinks, Ricci said, "We need to talk."

"I told you this morning, I'm really sorry. It won't happen again." She took a gulp from her chardonnay.

Ricci cocked his head. "Not about that. About Jez. Jez and me. We were married."

Dace swallowed another swig of wine. She nodded. "Brandon said something about that."

Ricci was quiet for a moment, swirling his wine in the glass, then said, "She was—is—my oldest friend's sister. Brandon is that friend, of course. I've known Jez for a long time. I spent a lot of time at their house hanging out with Brandon. When I was ten, she was two. She was always around, when we were kids and when we got older. She was familiar. It made sense at the time. I wanted to settle down, and she wanted me. I loved her, or so I thought at the time. She was—is—a free spirit; she was open and willing to experiment in, well, shall we say, conjugal relations. We did that a lot. Experimented. It was pretty great. I thought it would get us through our differences. It didn't. She said I was spiritually close-minded and that I was suffocating her. She left me, then wanted to come back. I said no." He took a drink of his wine.

For a moment, Dace felt pity for Jez, flying off on an impulse then realizing she still loved Ricci, but finding the door closed when she tried to return. She released her grip on her wineglass and rested her forearms on the table, her palms flat on either side of the sugar and creamer holder. "Did you ever feel regret about saying no?"

"Regret, no; guilt, yes. She really seemed to go off the new-age deep end after that. She got on this kick about veils between worlds and the beings who waited on the other side. She started the descents, as she calls them, about that time. She was teaching a writing course at the university called 'In the Land Between Heartbeats: Stories of Descent.' She still is, and, for a time, it became very popular among new agers. Then enrollments started dropping. She took the part-time job at Oblation Station, and started offering descents, a term she borrowed from an ancient story of transformation, the myth of Inanna, I think she said, promising participants they would make contact with beings from other times and worlds. I feel some responsibility that things have gotten to this point. If things spin further out of control, I'll feel even more responsible."

"I understand how that feeling can drive a person."

Ricci played with the sugar packets in their plastic box. "Were you ever married?" he asked.

Dace inched her hands closer to the sugar packets. "Once for about fifteen minutes."

As Ricci lifted sugar packets out and dropped them back in, his fingers brushed against hers. With each feathery stroke, arousal swirled deep in Dace's pelvis. She let her hands receive the gentle bump and stroke of Ricci's hands. "We dropped out of college our sophomore year to live on the beaches of North Carolina. We thought it would be easier to be married to do that, so we did, in a quickie civil service, no family. Not exactly a union built on solid foundations. My dad, as you know, a former fighter jet pilot, Navy, and respected local businessman, got it annulled." Dace pulled her hands away from Ricci's as a jolt of memory shot through her. "Oh my God, how did I forget. Did you and my dad have an arrangement, some sort of quid quo pro? Something that could be considered unethical or even illegal in business or on a job with a government contract?"

He drew back. He frowned. "No," he said. "Why would you ask that?"

"When you called with your resignation from the project, I was in his office. I'd gone there to resign. In your phone call, he asked you if your arrangement was still in place. Earlier, Brandon had implied the reason you two got the contract was a favor for a favor—Jez was supposed to help my mom get a job at Oblation Station." Dace's throat tightened as tears welled. She gripped the table's edge.

He slid his forearms along the tablecloth toward her hands, gently pried them off the edge and took them in his. "Your father was worried because your mother was worried. She said she felt something approaching you. Your dad asked me as a personal favor to keep an eye on you as you worked on the project."

Dace's tears spilled over and her face crumpled. She yanked her hands away from Ricci. "All of this," she said in a choked voice as swept out her arm, "and this morning was about keeping me safe?"

He reached into his pocket and handed her a neatly folded white handkerchief. "No, Dace. What you felt, or what I think you felt, I felt too, not just this morning but my first day in the office when your dad introduced us."

Dace dabbed her eyes with shaking hands. "What?" she managed to croak out.

"When your dad asked if our arrangement was still in place this morning on the phone, I told him I was interested in you. If he wanted me to continue with our informal arrangement that I'd keep you from harm, I told him he had to be comfortable with the fact I also wanted to see you. If you wanted to see me, of course. I don't think the situation violates any ethical rules."

"Why didn't you ask me out if you were interested after the first time we met?"

Ricci raised an eyebrow. "Is this a test? If so, the answer's easy: since at that time I was a contractor with your dad's firm, asking out an employee of said firm would have been a conflict of interest."

"For that, you get an A+," Dace said.

A corner of Ricci's mouth turned up in a grin.

Dace slid her hands from Ricci's gentle clasp and covered his hands in hers. In turn, he lightly stroked his warm, rough knuckles back and forth along her palms.

"Let's go," Dace whispered.

They rose. Ricci paid the bill, and they walked together into the Virginia evening and the blaze of the setting sun.

At her car, Ricci again took both of her hands, and, holding them, bent his head to kiss her, a firm, warm, lingering press of his lips against hers.

Dace wavered like an unsteady candle flame.

"Are you all right?" Ricci asked, pulling her close to his him.

Dace's legs shook. She nodded into his shoulder. "I live nearby. Follow me?"

Regretting her choice of underwear, Dace drove the short distance home with Ricci behind her.

At her apartment, she shyly took his suit coat and hung it over a high stool pushed against the counter. Ricci tugged off his tie.

"Be right back," Dace whispered.

In the bathroom, she released her hair from the tie and her hair spread in ripples around her shoulders. She slipped her top over her head, pulled off the sports bra then put the top back on. Before returning to the living room, she swapped out the beige undies for a scant G-string.

They stood facing each other in the small living room with no lights turned on, just the light of the almost-full moon. Ricci ran his fingertips down the sides of her face, neck, arms. His hands settled on her waist.

As he leaned in to kiss her, another face slid over his: the snake-eyed man. Dace gasped and jumped back.

"What's wrong?" Ricci asked, his forehead creasing in concern.

Dace shook her head and stepped back into Ricci's arms. "I'm seeing things. I thought I saw someone else's face slide over yours. Maybe it was a trick of the light." She looked at the black, gray, and white tones of the moonlight on the surfaces of objects in her dark apartment. She turned back to Ricci who pulled her tightly against him. The contours of her body pressed against his, and this time when she pressed against his hard-on, he pressed back.

His phone rang. He pulled back to look at the LCD. He answered it with one hand, the other around Dace's waist.

He spoke to the caller in one-word sentences: "What? When? Why?"

Dace slipped out of his embrace and sat on the couch, watching him in profile as he spoke. Again, the snake-eyed man's face seemed to slide into place over his features.

"That was Brandon." He put his jacket back on and pocketed his tie. His face was his own again. "I have to go," he said. "I'm so sorry. But I have to go."

He stood near the door, his arms hanging at his sides.

Dace rose, stepped to him and encircled his waist with her arms. "Can you come back?"

He kissed her lightly. "I don't know. Brandon says Jez is in trouble."

Still dopey with desire, Dace frowned in puzzlement. "What?" she asked, confused.

"I'll call you as soon as this is taken care of," he said, fishing in his trouser pocket for his car fob, and, finding it, kissed her one last time before he left, closing the door behind him.

For a few moments, Dace could not move from where she stood. She returned to the couch and sat there in the dark. Her body felt languid, awash in arousal, but her mind was stunned by the shock of Ricci's sudden departure to help Jez.

The moon's light filtered in through the window. The trembling leaves of the silver maple outside her window softly tapped against the panes.

I'm here, she heard.

A sound of breath filled Dace's right ear. As the breath moved rhythmically in and out, like a conch shell weaving toward then away, the maple leaves slowed their quivering then stopped, the breathing next to her ear inhaled and exhaled, rising into peaks and falling into valleys. The breathing abruptly moved away, though still hovering nearby. She passed her hand through the air next to her. Her hand tingled. Mesmerized, she held it there.

The breathing edged farther away, and the tingling stopped. "Light as a feather," came the thought, the chant that was supposed to levitate another a girl during a slumber party séance.

"You want me to hold a slumber party?" Dace whispered to the breathing presence. It moved to the opposite side of the room.

"No?" she said, when the breath stayed where it was. "Do you want me to stay light, take a light-hearted approach?" The breath didn't budge.

Images of the tiny, white feathers the snake-eyed man had blown out of his didgeridoo in her dream filled her mind. Then she understood: the snake-eyed man was trying to enter her world in his physical form.

The moment she thought that, the breath moved closer to her. The breath settled in close to her ear, lifting, releasing. Its volume lowered but the breath still pulsed near her. The maple leaves resumed their shaking, as though time had been reinstated.

Dace's phone in her pocket pinged. In her mind's eye, Ricci stepped through a door Brandon held open. Ricci checked his wristwatch then stood stiffly while Brandon's arms waved, gesturing at the walls. Then a wave of emotion came off Ricci and rolled toward Dace. It broke over her, flooding her with emotion and images: Ricci alone on a windswept moor, trying to find the way home, to her. Tears came to her eyes, and she blinked them away.

In her vision, Ricci joined Brandon who peered at scrawls of red writing at his eye level. He motioned for Ricci to look closer. Her view switched to a close up of Ricci. He craned his neck to look up at the writing, and the snake-eyed man's transparent face dropped over Ricci's. Then the ghostly mask disappeared from the face that had quickly grown dear to her.

A chill tingled along Dace's collarbone and picked up speed and power as it rolled down her spine. An electrical current shot into her sacrum and traveled to the racetrack of pelvic floor muscles. A sharp "Oh" escaped her.

The breathing man returned. He matched the rhythm of her inhales and exhales. Then there he was at her ear, and this time she felt his head-to-toe presence kneeling beside her as she sat on the couch. For a moment she glimpsed the barest outline of a face as the image rippled in the air. It was the snake-eyed man. He pulled her breath into the rhythm of his, and she slid into his eddy of invisible waves as a strong wind shook the leaves of the maple tree.

"Go," he whispered.

Dace felt a whooshing around her that pulled her off the couch. She was propelled to the door and her hand found the knob. "Wait!" she cried and grabbed her bag with her keys. Once she was out the door, it shut behind her, locking, and she ran down the stairs and out the main door into the night, guided by the light of the autumn moon and the whispering man.

Chapter 11
It Begins

DACE SWUNG OPEN THE CAR door and slid behind the wheel while the invisible man opened the passenger side door, and she assumed from the sound of weight settling into the leather seat, got in. Dace started the car and took off down the street.

"Ahn," he said. "Ahn-yees."

"Agnes?" Dace asked.

A wave of agreement surrounded her like a spray of cologne. She turned right onto an entrance ramp.

"Oblation Station it is," Dace said as she accelerated.

In the glow of the dashboard lights, the barest hint of his outline shown, his mane of hair thick and bound at the nape and the scant rise of his nose. His dark eyes glinted. He was still transparent, though, the leather car seat showing through his body clad in a dun-colored shift.

"Yes," he said.

"You can speak," Dace said, too dumbfounded to do anything but state the obvious as she sped onto the freeway.

"Do you have a name?" she asked.

"Beattakuka," he sang. His voice grew richer and deeper by

the moment.

"Again, please? Slower?"

"Bee-ah." He sang two tones, the second syllable higher. He continued on a note in the middle of the two then dropped down and back up: "ta-tu-ka."

"Bee-ah," Dace began then hesitated. She'd already forgotten the next syllable. "Can you repeat the last part?"

"Beatt," he said, pronouncing it flatly.

"Bee-ought," Dace said, sounding it out. "Okay, Beatt it is."

He shook his head, either, Dace imagined, acknowledging the effort of speaking her language or the sadness of hearing his name without any music.

Dace! she shouted to herself. *Pull it together. What are you getting yourself into? Or worse, what are you imagining?*

Then it dawned on her: these were her father's thoughts. Never before had she been able to find that space between her own thinking, her true beliefs, and her father's. The space grew as her thoughts shifted to Ricci. *Ricci*, she called out silently.

The wanting and the unknowing was too much. Dace shut down thoughts about Ricci. Instead, she wedged herself into the gap that had opened up in her mind where free thoughts—her own thoughts—roamed.

They reached the gates of Oblation Station. Dace jumped out of the car and pushed the gates open, the hinges squealing. She drove through then put the car in Park and ran back and pushed the gate closed.

Dace parked, and in the light of the waxing moon they found their way to the front door. As Beatt raised his translucent fist to knock, the door opened, and light spilled out onto Dace and through Beatt.

"Come in, my darlings," said Agnes, bent over her sparkly blue walker just inside the door. She twisted her gray-haired head up to smile at them. "I've been waiting for you."

Chapter 12
A Blow to the Soul

"FIRST OF ALL," AGNES BEGAN, "there isn't any governing body or council for all this, the sort of thing you see in novels and movies. I'll tell you what I've worked out based on my own experience and what I've learned from others I've encountered along the way. Cocoa?"

Dace shook her head. She sat next to Beatt on the couch in Agnes' study. Only a small oil lamp burned, casting a soft light on the three of them.

"God didn't make it easy," Agnes continued. "Bit of a tease sometimes. He got intelligence, emotions, and instincts all into matter but left it up to us to figure out how to undo it all and become like him or whatever pronoun you choose to use. Your people," she inclined her head toward Beatt, "understood it much better than we do."

"The void," Beatt said.

"What's that, dear?" Agnes asked.

Puzzled, Dace repeated, "The void."

Agnes nodded. "Ah yes, the void. The place to undo yourself and become God, really, intelligence dispersed like water droplets."

Beatt leaned forward, glittering. "We accessed the void with our bodies. Our women of hieros house held the knowledge and transmitted it to those not allowed to hold it."

"I apologize," Agnes said, "Your voice sounds like a burbling stream to me. Rather nice, but I can't quite make out what you're saying. Dace?"

"He said, people of his time used their bodies but only certain women actually had the knowledge." Dace turned to Beatt. "Used their bodies? Um, how, exactly?"

He gestured to the area between his legs then to the same area between Dace's. Dace blushed and shrank into her corner of the couch.

"Oh!" Agnes exclaimed. "Yes, of course, sex. Sacred sex. But only these certain women could actually possess the knowledge?"

Sacred what? screamed in Dace's mind. *Are we talking prostitutes? Am I getting involved in something illegal? What would Meladee do?* If her brave and bold friend were in her place, how would she handle this situation?

Dace translated for Beatt. To her it sounded as though she were using Agnes' exact words, but Beatt could not understand them when they came out of Agnes' mouth.

"Yes," Beatt answered, "the women of hieros house. They punished anyone who figured it out for themselves."

"Oh dear," murmured Dace, then repeated what he'd said.

Agnes considered. "And now anyone can have the ability, though, as I say, it's along a spectrum. And sex isn't required."

Dace's face reddened. "Maybe it is. Or at least some aspect. After my descent, when I woke in my room, the face of man I'm attracted to appeared above me then turned in to what I now realize was Beatt's face. And then tonight, when I was on a date with this man, Ricci, Beatt's face appeared to float over Ricci's while we were, um… kissing." Her face burned.

"Hm," Agnes pondered. "Can you ask Beatt how all these elements fit together to have brought him at least partly into our world?"

Dace repeated Agnes' question. Beatt shook his head.

"Until we can define this new process," Agnes said, "we may have to rely on the old one: a blow to the soul, an experience that shocks an individual out of their regular life, or what they think their regular life is."

"Agnes, sorry, but I don't understand," Dace said.

"Have you ever fallen in love fast and hard?" asked Agnes.

Dace blushed. Had Agnes read her mind?

"I'll take that a yes." Agnes smiled. "It's a version of the jolt that I'm referring to, though, in truth, a kinder whammy that many experience. The blow to my soul was the moment I realized my curving spine was permanent and I would never raise my head to the visual glories of God again. I was lost for so long, my head forced to look down at the dirt instead of the sun. The prioress handed me a broom and for a long time I swept and cried. Slowly, and I don't know exactly how, observing the ground put spaces in my anger and despair. As those feelings lightened, I discovered I could sense things going on in the soil—growth, death, decay and that was the beginning of learning about new worlds for me." Agnes paused. "That was many years ago. Things have developed quite a bit since then, as you two have demonstrated."

Agnes' words echoed in Dace's mind: lost; cried; despair; space. *Sounds like love to me,* thought Dace. Ricci returned to her mind, and her body reached out to him with tendrils of yearning. *Ricci,* she called again silently. Nothing answered her. *It's me and the broom,* she thought. *I'm right where I should and deserve to be: with a former nun planning some sort of paranormal revolution and a half-formed guy from another time who only I can understand.*

"Beatt," Agnes said abruptly, "we need to get you in some less conspicuous clothing." She rose and pushed her walker to the study closet and rummaged in the drawer of a chest inside. "Ah," she said, "here we are." She handed him a t-shirt and a pair of trousers then a pair of canvas slip-ons. "These belonged to one of the trimmer sisters. Her clothes should fit you, more or less. Not sure about the shoes, but let's see."

Both Agnes and Dace turned discreetly away as Beatt changed. When the rustling of fabric had quieted, both turned around.

He turned back the placket of the pants to expose the hollow inside of the top snap, revealing a thin trail of dark pubic hair.

The color rose in Dace's cheeks. "Sort of lay one metal piece on top of the other and squeeze them together," she said, miming the action.

He lay the hollow top against its mate and with thumb and forefinger pressed the two together until an audible click sounded. He looked up, smiled, then finished fastening his trousers and straightened the fabric of his T-shirt. Both his trousers and shirt sparkled and lost their definition as they melded into Beatt.

He sat back down on the couch and Dace joined him. He leaned against Dace as he pulled on the canvas shoes. She felt only the slightest of pressure, as though a draft wafted against her.

"Why do you have to be undone to access the void?" Dace asked. "And how does that happen?"

In the muted light, Agnes' deeply curved neck resembled that of a swan. She inclined her head to look at Beatt and Dace.

"The ability, for us humans, anyway, takes places on a

continuum," Agnes said. "On one end, you have people born with no or few boundaries. Your mother, Dace, is one of these."

Dace sat quietly. Dace had her own opinions about her mother's lack of boundaries. To Dace, the lack was systemic; it pervaded every part of her mother, emotional, mental, spiritual and physical. Her mother had no barrier between herself and the outer world, always expressing everything she was feeling and had on her mind. When it came to her beliefs, that there are other realms and beings which populate them—and Dace was now feeling forced to grant those beliefs credence—it was as though her mother believed her body was a ruse, and without thinking she easily transcended it.

"You've met her?"

"Yes, I met her when she came by to pick up an application," Agnes continued. "I had a chance to talk with her a bit. She's very open about how she experiences the two worlds. She's unusual in that she has no layers between what she is in this world and what she was born to do: function as a gateway for energies and entities transforming from one dimension to another."

Dace felt stunned hearing another speak of what her mother believed in and finding nothing to doubt about it. All these years Dace had adopted her father's gently scoffing stance toward her mother. Dace had hidden and squelched her abilities similar to her mother's so he would never view her that way or that she would feel the sting of not being taken seriously. But that had never bothered her mother. Dace marveled at what must be a strong and unerring faith her mother possessed in her nature. Dace's respect for her mother blossomed, and a bud of regard opened for her own well-buried nature.

Agnes continued: "Unlike your mother, most with this ability layer a role over it. The layers function as disguised stand-ins for what the individuals are called to do in the spirit world. The layer probably looks like perfection in the practice of a craft or profession. The individual probably feels driven to be perfect at what they do, whatever it is, and to always be doing it."

"Always be working, always be perfect." Dace repeated her work mantra softly as realization dawned.

Agnes nodded. "Pristine calibration. Transforming entities requires constant work and constant perfection. I was surprised when you showed up to substitute for your mother, Dace. I also never expected Jez' descent to actually have results. I see now it was providence. You just needed a nudge for the layer to dissolve."

Dace took umbrage. "My mother has arthritis. She could have never managed Jez' set-up to hang upside down. Or if she did, she could have hurt herself."

Agnes patted her hand. "I would have never let it get that far. I just needed a pretense to get your mother here to talk more with her and request she assist us. In my own reading of Jungians like Sylvia Brinton Perera, I had ideas about how I could recreate the process without the props and move beyond the first stage of manifesting other-worldly energies to the second, where actual beings are transformed." She nodded at Beatt.

"You could have just offered her a job," Dace noted.

Agnes shook her head. "An unneeded layer. Besides, Moore Electric let me know a few days ago they've instituted a hiring freeze until we have more revenue coming in. I'm hoping Jez's descents will create that revenue."

Dace sat awash in conflicting feelings. She could not let go of her grudge against Jez but her new-found admiration for her mother pushed her to consider larger possibilities. She looked down at Beatt's twinkling hand resting on the couch cushion then raised her eyes. He pulsed bright then dim like a new star and met her gaze with a smile. *New worlds*, she repeated silently to herself. She couldn't leave him in this state of half transformation.

"There's no other way to see beings in different dimensions or move through dimensions unless you receive this blow to the soul?" Dace asked.

Agnes nodded. "I believe so, for the time being. It needn't be violent, just something that takes you out of everyday life. Grief can do that. Loss and depression work well too. Once you are taken out of what you call your life, your attention turns inward. Imagination with a capital "I" develops, or what a mystic born in the 1300s in Spain named Ibn 'Arabi called 'active Imagination.' Active Imagination is the function that is tied to another realm that objectively exists. But you can't access it with your normal senses. You must use active Imagination. It's actually quite simple but these days difficult. Science sent imagination to its room and never let it back out."

Dace recalled Brandon's thought experiments. "Not entirely."

"Well, that would be news to me," commented Agnes. "I believe it's up to those of us who don't disregard the obvious truths: that if you pay attention—that is, you don't dismiss something you imagine coming true as coincidence or think 'just a dream' when you encounter messages and entities during sleep or when awake—the barrier between begins to dissolve. Over time the way your vision works changes and you start to see creatures. Beatt saw you, Dace, and you saw Beatt. And others that are the results of various experiments, you might say." Agnes quietly took a sip of her cocoa.

Beatt straightened. Dace looked at him as the muted light sparkled through his frame. His eyes glistened with emotion; perhaps empathy for Agnes, something Dace was also feeling.

Agnes caught the charge of the emotion passing between Beatt and Dace. "Oh, darlings, no, I'm not an experiment, nor am I from another world. I'm just an old, hunchbacked oblate, forever in-between."

"An oblate who guards the portal into other worlds," Dace added.

Agnes laughed. "Well, I suppose you could say that. Though Beatt is my first to have transformed so fully. Those who transformed as mostly energy and just a touch of solidity sank back very quickly from whence they came."

"There really is a veil between worlds that can be lifted and dropped?" Dace asked. "Just like Jez says?"

"It's best to let some think so. It's a simple construct that won't frighten anyone, and it takes any attention off those of us doing this work. Though as I'm sure you are aware hardly anyone pays attention to nuns and oblates." Agnes gazed off into the darkness beyond the windows of her study. "There is such power in being ignored."

Dace's heart thudded with the memory of how it felt when Ricci had left so suddenly to run to the aid of Jez. He appeared in her mind's eye as he stood near the door just before he left: his steady gaze, his arms hanging awkwardly at his side. Then she remembered: Brandon had loaded the GEOV app to her phone. She pulled her phone out of her bag and powered it off. "Agnes," Dace said, leaning forward, "Brandon, Jez' brother, will be able to find me. He's on contract with my dad's company and I've got his app on my phone." She held up her device. "I just shut it down but he may have already detected where I am. I mean, that's fine, but do you really want people here right now?"

Agnes nodded in acknowledgement.

"Jezebel," Agnes called out in her tremulous voice, "It's time."

Dace's eyes widened and her jaw dropped as one wall of Agnes' study creaked open, and Jez slipped into the room, her eyes blazing.

"Jez, this is Dace Banks and—" Agnes began.

"Yes, I know," she said abruptly. "The boss' daughter. Nice to meet you. Isn't it exciting?" she gushed, spinning in a little circle before Agnes' chair wearing a beige shift with a head scarf tied at her nape, her lush hair cascading down her back.

Dace could only gape. Beatt rippled beside her.

"You must get into position, dear," said Agnes, leaning on her walker and pulling herself to her feet. "I know we expect your brother but I'm guessing Ricci will be along as well. We're also expecting a good showing from your followers, the white-veiled descenders."

The space that had opened up in Dace's thinking snapped shut. Shame filled her as though she were facing the prospect of her father discovering the nonsense she was taking part in and then collided with a fresh fear that ripped through her: would Ricci choose Jez over her when he witnessed Jez' spectacle? If she left now, she could just get home by the time Jez's stunt was over and Ricci might call her.

"Agnes," she began.

"I'm ready," Jez said, cutting Dace off.

Jez stood tall and threw her shoulders back as though she were Joan of Arc on her way to the stake. Jez turned to Dace. Her head was haloed by her swaths of dark hair in the backlight of the oil lamp. "No one will doubt my ability to lift veils between worlds after this. When word gets out I returned from the void, the world will know descent and veils are real. The U won't cancel my class, and Harper Row will publish my book."

"Yes, dear, now come along," Agnes said as she aimed her walker at the doorway and gestured for Jez to go ahead of her.

Jez spun on her heel and fluttered out like a ballerina on pointe.

"Wait for me in the reception area, dear," Agnes called to her. Agnes turned to Dace and the flickering Beatt whose diamond-shaped pupils shone like stars in clouds.

"You not only know about Jez' hoax but you're helping her?" Dace asked Agnes, incredulous. "I don't think I can be a part of this. She's deceiving a lot of people. Doesn't that mean you are too? A nun who lies?"

"A former nun who lies," Agnes corrected. She sagged against her walker. "I'm sorry, Dace. I know the situation can seem black and white in terms of right and wrong, but these circumstances are far more gray than you realize. We are so close to being able to bring people and beings from previous times, when the void was understood, into our time, allowing us to complete our missing selves. There are parts within us that know how to go into the void, like the women of heiros house could do in Beatt's time. We can end the need for blows to the soul just to become one with the other-worldly, to become psychologically whole. Imagine the ramifications."

Dace's head swam with visions of Ricci's departing back in her apartment after the phone call from Brandon and the emotional searing she had experienced. Was Agnes right? Was it possible to restore some old knowledge to people in current times that could end emotional suffering? Her imagined scene switched to the look of disbelief and disapproval her father would surely cast at her if she tried to explain this to him. Even more farfetched, what was the chance he would understand that if she didn't help, Beatt might dwindle away and maybe, but maybe not, go back to whence he came? Meladee popped in next, saying *What? You left before the rest of the adventure occurred?* and stood shoulder to shoulder with her mother who beamed with joy as Dace made her fondest wish come true.

Agnes straightened and placed her outstretched hand on Dace's. "Your mother went through her own blow to the soul."

The only extraordinary encounter her mom wouldn't elaborate on was the one that turned her inside out, as she put it. She offered mainly the mundane details and only a smidgen of those more unusual. She was eighteen, and it was the summer before she would start college at Old Dominion University in nearby Norfolk. She lived with her parents in their home on 85th Street in Virginia Beach, a block from the ocean front. Her older sister was interning for the summer and living in Arlington. Life at home was more peaceful without her but the second floor of their home where the girls' bedrooms were located felt empty without her sister's combination of acerbic remarks when Rowena innocently revealed her clairvoyance and advice about makeup and men. *In thirty-five days I'm starting college*, she thought as she lay down to sleep one night in her quiet upper storey bedroom. The moon was new, and no lunar light shone in her room through the sheers. She plummeted into a deep slumber and found herself approaching a series of gates. She proceeded through each of the seven gates and at each was stripped of a piece of clothing after which a force took her up into the "mother ship." And there ended her story, at least the one she told Dace.

"She told you? The entire story?" Dace readied herself to feel hurt that her mother spilled all to someone she barely knew.

Agnes nodded. "Only a bit, but that was all I needed in

order to understand."

Dace's emotional armor softened. Her mother had probably shared the same details with Agnes.

Agnes continued. "She said she was no longer who she used to be and not yet where she was going. I knew the depth of loss behind such a statement. She never fully regained her footing in this world. She told me it was a blessing when she met your father. Dace, without that blow to the soul, there wouldn't have been a place in your mother's life for your father to fit into, which he did rather perfectly. Your descent resulted in the same perfect symmetry. You and Beatt fit together like two puzzle pieces."

Not the soul mate I had in mind, thought Dace, feeling the sadness of her brief time with Ricci.

"You'll help us, won't you? Help Beatt continue metamorphosing into our world? Save others from never having go through what your mother and you did?"

Dace felt whatever was once herself had been pulverized into bits. But she didn't yet feel or believe she wasn't who she used to be or didn't know where she was going. Well, maybe the latter; her internal rudder wasn't working but that didn't mean it wouldn't again. Staying attentive to the job at hand had always saved her, even if all those jobs had come from her father, whether working at his company or joining him in keeping Mom safe.

"How will this help my mother?"

"As soon as Moore Electric lifts the hiring freeze, I'll offer her a job. I can also offer her a sympathetic ear to her blow to her soul, as someone who has also experienced it. You never really get over it. I can show her how to bring her experience into the light, incorporate it into the self."

"Will you make sure Jez gets rid of that ridiculous hammock?"

Agnes nodded. "Descent in the hammock will be optional.

I've supplied Jez with necessary knowledge to guide others on a metaphorical descent. Jez has nearly completed the course that will use such a figurative experience to teach people how to enter the void using their minds and not their bodies. She'll tell people she discovered this on her most recent descent in which she accidentally accessed the void. She need not reveal I helped her with the approach. Whatever Jez realizes personally as benefits will, in the larger scheme, be like the proverbial drop of water in a bucket while Oblation Station will, I hope, thrive and, hidden from view, carry on transformations such as Beatt's."

"All right," Dace said grimly, sealing her fate in this process. *Who am I becoming?* she asked herself rhetorically. A pinprick of light flickering on the surface of her forearm caught her eye.

"You and Beatt can be a part of this," Agnes said. "Please come with us."

Beatt rose.

"Wait," said Dace, standing. "You and I can see Beatt but I don't think Jez could see him. He also seems to have some effect on clothing or anything that is against his person. The closer a thing or maybe a person gets to him, it or they become less invisible. You can see and hear him but can't make out what he's saying. I can both see and understand him. There's no way to know who will and won't be able to see him." Dace paused for a moment, thinking. "Maybe it has to do with where a person is on the spectrum you mentioned earlier?"

"You may be right. For now, we'll be cautious." She pointed to a broom in the corner. "Thank goodness for Elizabeth's forgetfulness. If you'll bring that broom along, Dace, I'll show you how we can use it as a prop."

Agnes wheeled out the door, and Dace and Beatt followed.

In the center atrium, dimly lit with sconces, Agnes stationed Beatt in a corner and placed the broom in his hands. Jez hung limply on the reception desk.

"I've conjured a janitor," Agnes said. "Another wholly ignored set of people."

Dace smiled in spite of herself.

Thumping on the door sounded, along with muffled shouts.

Elizabeth appeared next to Agnes in her robe and slippers. "Agnes, good heavens, what's going on?" she asked.

"Can I ask that you trust me that what is happening will be good for the Station, and good for us?" Agnes asked. "With a promise to explain tomorrow?"

Elizabeth's brow furrowed then relaxed and she set her jaw. "All right," she said. "I want what's good for the Station."

"Can you handle crowd control?" Agnes asked her.

She nodded and tightened the fabric belt of her robe, girding for battle.

"Ready?" Agnes whispered, looking back and forth between Elizabeth and Jez.

Jez, eyes aflame, nodded.

"Elizabeth, will you unlock the door?"

As Elizabeth scuffed toward the door, Dace whispered to Agnes, "I don't think Elizabeth could see Beatt."

Agnes nodded without taking her eyes away from Elizabeth. "I thought that might be the case."

When Elizabeth turned the latch and drew back the door, Brandon bounded in followed by a passel of Jez's followers, somewhere around thirty, Dace guessed. The descenders wore delicate white veils that trembled over their faces, and all held their phones at the ready.

"Jez," Brandon shouted and rushed to her side. "You're safe."

The veiled women crowded in and called out Jez' name

in soft wails. They took selfies then snapped pictures of Jez collapsing into her brother's arms. Agnes edged back to stand in the corner with Beatt and Dace.

Ricci burst through the open door. Dace's heart leapt and her body instinctively moved toward him. Beatt's glow flamed up and he pressed himself to Dace's side.

Ricci's eyes darted around the atrium. Finding Dace, he pushed past the crush of veiled women as Agnes edged away, back into the shadows of the corridor.

Like Beatt's clothing, Dace's substantiality began to fade. She opened her mouth to call to Ricci but no sound came out.

Ricci stood before Dace. His tie was loosened into a cowl, and the front of his hair was brushed erratically onto his forehead.

"Dace, why are you here?" he asked, his eyes searching hers. "I went back to your apartment. When I didn't find you there, I used the GEOV app to locate you."

Beatt shrouded her in his essence which was as sparkly as silica. Dace felt the connection to Ricci falter. She stared out at him as though from inside a snow globe. She felt confused and could not summon words.

He looked around. "I don't understand why you're here."

His words were muffled as though she heard them from behind thick glass. She could not organize her thinking to form words.

He shook his head. "Never mind. I can't make any sense of this right now. Will you come with me?" He stepped closer, and his vibration bubbled toward her and broke over her body.

Ricci's laser-like gaze pulled her toward him a few inches. Beatt once again enveloped her with his essence and she teetered backwards. Ricci lunged to grab her, but his arms encountered air and he stumbled then righted himself.

His face flushed in confusion. "What's going on, Dace?"

"Jack? Ready to go?" Brandon called from across the lobby. He stood outside the circle of women entwined around Jez.

"Dace?" Ricci tried one last time.

Beatt showered Dace in glittery, zinging bits, like crushed particles of bullets. The metallic sprinkles hardened into a shell around her.

Ricci rolled his shoulders forward, as though protecting his heart, and turned away from Dace. With a heavy step, he joined Brandon, and they followed Jez and her believers out of Oblation Station.

Beatt maintained his energetic caul around Dace.

"The time has come," called Jez, and then she was gone.

Ricci, Dace implored silently.

Ricci hesitated on the threshold. Beatt revved like an engine. Ricci did not turn, then continued out the door.

Chapter 13
Home is Oblation

BEATT VIBRATED NEXT TO DACE. Agnes rolled back to them, and she leaned toward Dace. Dace was bookended by Agnes' surprising outpouring of warmth and Beatt's electrical tingles which seemed to be re-wiring her brain and emotions. Ricci's name felt foreign in her mind. *Ree-chee*, she thought; *what kind of name is that?*

Elizabeth called out from the doorway, "All are welcome to return tomorrow and descend."

She shut the door, locked it, and turned to face Agnes and Dace. "Well," she said.

"Good work, Elizabeth," Agnes said, wheeling toward her. "Thank you."

"You're welcome," she said with a little bow. "But I'm not entirely comfortable with all the mystery. I look forward to tomorrow's complete reveal."

"Can I ask you to do one more thing? See which two retreatants' rooms are available? One for Dace, the other for—" she hesitated. "Just in case."

"Of course," Elizabeth said and sailed off down the hallway.

Agnes rolled back to Dace and Beatt. She placed her hand on Dace's arm. "The kitchen helpers put aside rice and apple crisp for us. Do you think you could chop vegetables to have with the rice?"

Her memory of Ricci standing before her rapidly faded like a fleeting dream image. *I guess this is the new me*, she thought, fated to be in service to the void. She was becoming the nun her mom had always wanted to be. "Yes," she said. She leaned into Beatt's light, peering into his face that now shimmered without his feed cap. "Do you eat?"

He laughed. "I can try."

Dace turned to Agnes, covering her hand with hers. "How do you like your vegetables done?"

Agnes pressed her slight frame against Dace's arm. "Just broth for me, dear. I have some in a thermos in my office. Tomorrow's Friday. I have some work to do for the end-of-week service. You two go ahead. The kitchen is on this level. Just follow the green stripe on the floor."

With a final squeeze of her warm hand and a nod, Agnes made her way down the hall to her office, her sparkly blue walker sliding along the floor.

Dace chopped vegetables. Beatt stood next to her and twinkled like the inside of a geode.

They ate in the Station's empty dining room, lit only by the emergency exit sign leading to the garden and the moon hanging low in the sky.

Beatt took an experimental forkful.

"I can eat!" he said, laughing, as his form wavered like heat waves on tarmac.

"What did you—do you—eat usually?" Dace's mind swirled. Talking was hard without tenses.

"Fruit, barley. Dried fruit after harvest and until next

season. If I can keep the fire going long enough in winter, roasted root vegetables." He paused. "But that was before."

"Before...."

"Before the Gigante overran Dia and the half-and-halfs joined the Ssha in the deepest layers of their cave and went into hibernation."

"Oh, I see." Dace did not see. She looked at her hands in her lap. She had always considered herself open-minded but apparently that was to new information about the known world. "I'm sorry, but I don't even know what most of your words mean."

He nodded. "I had the same feeling the first time Mave repeated some of the things the Gigante said in Apollonoulous."

"Apollo... like the Greek god? Wait, Mave?"

"Her full name is now Mavealeph, but I still call her Mave."

Dace's jaw unhinged. Muffaleph was the name of an alien being her mother thought she heard whispered during visits. *Undeniable evidence*, thought Dace, *or close enough*. Then she was flooded with regret. *All those years we tried to convince Mom none of it was real.* Her eyes filled.

"Are you sensing Mave's pain?" Beatt asked matter-of-factly. "I wouldn't be surprised if you were, given your connection with her. You were the only one who could consistently perceive her."

"Oh, Beatt, something's terribly wrong. I'm not the one Mave visited; that was my mother, Rowena."

"Ah, that was you on the beach."

"You're spindrift man?" Dace sputtered.

"I'm the one who connected with you on a beach then outside where you slept so very high up."

"Shouldn't you have connected with my mother?" Dace's eyes were wide in bafflement.

He shrugged liquidly. "Need summons need."

Dace blinked rapidly and shook her head. "Information overflow. Let's maybe not talk for a while."

In silence they put away the food, Dace giving Beatt the job of spooning leftovers into containers. While Dace washed the dishes, Beatt swept the floor. Afterwards they sat together on the stone steps outside the Station kitchen.

Dace's mind and emotions had calmed. She owed it to her mother to see this through.

"What happens next?" she asked.

He shifted so he faced her. Bits of him twinkled, as though he were covered in starlight.

"The hope is I continue to materialize in this world. Can you maintain functioning as a gateway?"

"I'm not sure. That 'pristine calibration' Agnes referred to was strong when I had a layer between my ability as a gateway and who I was in this world: always be working, always be perfect. My only concern is the what happens as my mental attitude shifts? What will happen to the ability with this shift? What will happen to you? That attitude was a well-honed habit; my mind, body, heart, soul and spirt all knew how to do it 24/7."

Beatt cocked his diaphanous head. "Twenty-four seven?"

She smiled. "All day, all night, all the time." She paused. "I should probably keep working at my day job as usual, at least until… we know that you're safe, one way or another."

Beatt nodded, like the undulating fabric of the star-studded sky.

Sitting on the concrete steps, the dirt beneath the soles of her sturdy shoes, energy rushed within her as her inner engine shifted gears, leaving behind the structures that had allowed her to cover up who she was. *All that time and attention squandered on keeping secrets*, she thought. Full, easy breaths expanded her rib cage, lifting up her chest, and a deep peace settled in the pit of her stomach. She looked down at her forearm and her thighs. They pulsed with an almost imperceptible glow, like a submerged jellyfish. This Beatt, who sat twinkling in the moonlight—was that an iridescent scale near his jaw?—had helped her become who she was. Something in her relaxed and settled. Somehow she was becoming more of herself yet at the same time becoming less a physical being in the known dimensions of the material world.

A faint beep sounded from her pocket. "How can that be," she said, pulling out her phone and looking at the LCD. "It's still off."

Beatt leaned against her, melded with her, really, to peer at the phone cradled in her palm. He looked up at Dace with utter confusion in his eyes.

"I'll explain later," she said, smiling.

They found a note from Elizabeth on the cutting board directing them to the retreatant rooms where they could spend the night.

Dace unlaced her Oxfords and padded down the quiet halls in her bare feet with Beatt rippling beside her. When they reached Dace's room, indicated by her name on a rectangular piece of paper inserted into a frame, and the one beside it with "available," she paused and looked at Beatt. Even though he wasn't fully matter she could see the outline of his leonine nose, just as she'd seen that moment when he'd manifested above her. But first Ricci had manifested. *Oh God*, she thought, *Ricci*. She leaned heavily against the door.

Beatt's eyes flickered with concern.

"This isn't going to be easy. The man I mentioned, Ricci, has had a powerful effect on me. I feel okay then once again I'm reduced to… I don't know what. I don't get it. I've transformed a being from another time into ours, I'm turning from solid into particle, and it's a very solid human man, Jack Ricci, who has the power to make my knees buckle. To go to pieces. To fall apart. To lose my words. To truly become something I wasn't before. To be someone undone by love. But it's not meant to be." She straightened. Lat, long, lat long, she said to herself. Straighten up and fly right. "Good night, Beatt," she said before he could say anything, his eyes full of compassion. Any more of that, she thought, and she'd dissolve into a glowing puddle. She entered her room. Then she stepped back out in the hall where Beatt still stood. "You turn the knob, that's what this is called, and the door opens," she said, demonstrating.

Beatt smiled, and his being lit up like the starry firmament. He slipped into his room and shut his door.

Dace went back to her room, also shutting the door. The attached bathroom supplied a plastic-wrapped toothbrush, toothpaste and pump soap. She brushed her teeth and washed her face. She hung her jeans over a chair and pulled off her top, took off her bra, then put her top back on and crawled into bed. She lay on her back, staring up at the ceiling then closing her eyes. She was flooded with the memory of Ricci kissing her, holding her tightly to his warm, hard body, the erotic pleasure of anticipating what was to come as they rocked against each other. What now would never come, she thought. She smiled sadly at her double entendre and fell asleep.

Chapter 14
The Gateway Opens

THE NEXT MORNING AT THE daily service Agnes gave a talk on God being found in the spiraling worms of the dirt then led the overflowing congregation in a period of silence while Dace and Beatt sat in the dining room. Dace sipped coffee.

"You'll function as a gateway for more than just me," Beatt said, his hand with its gleaming dots holding a piece of toast. He took a tentative bite. He'd solidified slightly more overnight and Dace could no longer see through him but he still remained diaphanous as did his clothing.

"You mean I should expect a parade of beings partially popping in without warning?"

He frowned as he negotiated another bite of toast, chewed, and swallowed. "I don't know what all those words mean, but I think I understand your question: will you have a choice in who or what transforms through you?"

"Exactly. Or will I be some sort of free-wheeling turnstile?"

He looked at her, puzzled. *Back to the parade of beings popping in and out*, she thought. She was probably the only girl who didn't have sex in high school and when she finally did in her first year of college, the fellow quickly became her boyfriend and, eventually, very short-term husband. "I'm not the sort of person who could handle a multitude making use of my gateway." She smiled at her joke. Beatt did not and instead sipped tea.

"Has anyone ever done this before?" Dace asked, taking a different tack.

"In old Dia, the women of hieros house did. But it was Ssha energy they transformed so that it found its place in physical forms, the people of Dia, animals, plants, all growing things. I never took part of the hieros house women's rituals since I had Ssha blood. Manifesting through you—with you—was my first experience in metamorphosis." He lightly touched her hand.

Dace withdrew her hand into her lap then looked questioningly up at him. "I've never heard of the hieros house women."

"You may have, but not by their original name. The invading Gigante renamed them House of Hor. They were holy women," he explained. "They had natural abilities but received training to transmit sacred knowledge the Ssha transmitted to them."

"The Ssha?"

"Giant lizard people who are—were—the source of our spirituality which revered the void, where you go to dissolve yourself and move like water droplets."

"Oh, dear. Giant lizard people, eh? That's going to take a while for me to absorb. Giant lizards? You're absolutely sure?"

He laughed. "I'm sure. Even in my time people had begun to forget they'd actually existed. They'd gone deep underground into their crystalline caves, in a kind of suspended state." He patted his lower back and shook his head. "I am from them. In my time, I have a tail. It hasn't come through yet."

"You realize I can never tell anyone any of this. No one would believe me."

"Jez Bell would."

"Jez Bell!" Dace exclaimed. The sound of Jez's name caused a tearing sensation in her heart, and a sadness came over her. How could one woman rend her life in so many ways?

"Did someone say my name?" a rich, throaty voice sang out. Jez stood in the dining room doorway, peering about expectantly. A young man in frayed denim and a loose T-shirt stood behind her with his hands in his pockets.

"Sit very still," Beatt whispered and put his glimmering arms around Dace.

The glow in her thighs broke into flecks and spread to both of her legs then swam up her torso, down to her fingertips and back up to her neck then to the top of her head. She tried to hang onto the thoughts that told her who she was but her consciousness dissipated and scattered in droplets.

"Huh. Thought I heard my name," Jez said. "Guess not." She stepped into the dining room and looked around. She took a large bite out of a pastry.

"Hey, I know," the young man said, trailing in after her, "maybe you're, like, picking up on all the mentions you're getting on social media."

"I like that. Note it. We can use it." She snapped her fingers. "That reminds me. I need to send my brother my phone info. He's going to use it in his testing of this new app he's working on—Geoff, something like that. Here, would you do it?" She handed her phone to Peter who bent his head to the device.

As Peter tapped and scrolled, Jez munched her pastry and looked idly around. She squinted into the corner where Beatt and Dace sat. A shaft of sunshine from a skylight beamed directly down on them. "What the—" she said.

"Okay, done. Hey, look at this," Peter interrupted, peering at his device. "Another 10,000 hits! Go hashtag descent!"

Jez whirled around, the tassels of her ponchos swinging from the centrifugal force. "What about hashtag Jez? How's that doing?"

"Mm," Peter murmured as he scrolled and tapped. He shook his head. "Don't see it in anyone's post."

Jez put her hands on her hips. "Gotta have hashtag Jez. Let everyone know to include it in all communications, social media, emails, whatever."

Peter furiously tapped on his phone. "Okay, emailed the group."

"Good. Thanks, Peter. Sorry, I get nervous that one small thing that goes wrong will bring this whole effort down. It's got to work. Can you double check we're doing everything possible to be sure my website comes up at the top in search results? And let me know if we've recruited bloggers who will write about me?"

"Good morning, Jez," Elizabeth sang out as she came into the dining room. Her nimbus of white hair surrounded her face. "I've been looking for you." She wore lavender knit pants, a white cotton shirt buttoned up the front with a Peter Pan collar, and over it a gray cardigan.

Jez rearranged her face from a worried frown to a happy smile, the corners of her mouth curling up. "Elizabeth, good morning," she chirped. "Peter and I are just discussing the descents on social media."

Elizabeth nodded to Peter then said, "That's exactly why I've been looking for you. We're full up with descent reservations! Callers are burning up the phone lines!"

"Praise be," Jez clasped her hands together and looked skyward. "It's happening. We're spreading the spiritual word."

"And filling up the coffers, if you don't mind me saying," Elizabeth said. "We have revenue targets from our corporate owners, Moore Electric, and I'm happy to say it seems very likely we'll be meeting them this month."

"Oh, I let you and the other oblates worry about worldly gains," Jez demurred, tucking her chin and lifting a shoulder. "My job is spirit and allowing others to experience the glories of the void to find their God."

Elizabeth tilted her head to the side. Peter's eyes grew wide.

"I mean find God," Jez amended. "Period. Just one God."

"Well," said Elizabeth brightly, "back to the phones. I need to relieve Miriam so she can help the kitchen volunteers put out the breakfast. Agnes' service will be done in a few minutes, and we've got a full house."

"Yes, and we've got work to do in my office," Jez said, and the three of them left the room.

Beatt's arms dropped away from Dace's shoulders like an ebbing wave. The blinking, bright flecks that she had coalesced into returned to a slight glow as she transitioned from particle back into somewhat more solid matter. She shook her head as though coming out of a trance. Beatt sat studying her.

"That's your ultimate state," he said. "Or what you'll become with me, eventually. That's what really happens when you're initiated into the void."

"I feel dazed," Dace said. "I sort of have a memory of Jez and Peter, and Elizabeth, but I'm not sure. Something's there but it's not knowledge that I feel in my body."

"When you're in this ultimate state, you essentially no longer have a body. That's why you don't feel the knowledge there. You—not exactly you, but particles that moved toward coalescing into you—had no physical place to implant the emotion and the memory."

Dace's gaze dropped to the beige carpet, a blank canvas that allowed her to take in Beatt's words. She raised her eyes. "Now I feel it in my body," she said. "I think about what we heard, and I feel anger and, well, a desire to do something not nice to Jez Bell."

Beatt rested his hand with its ridged fingernails that ended in a point on her forearm. "Best to let the natural course of things take care of Jez Bell," he said.

"Suddenly I have to move." She jumped up and stretched, then marched in place. "My body feels like ants have invaded." She stretched out her arms and tilted her head side to side, then angled her chin toward her armpit. She made a face. "Whew!" she said, laughing, "I'm stinky!" She swooped in to take a sniff of Beatt's flickering underarm. "Pardon me, but you are too!" she said.

"I'm becoming matter," he said.

Dace laughed. "You're mattering," she said. "We should go to my place for fresh clothes for me and the nearest men's clothing store for you."

They found Agnes working in her office and Dace told her of their plans.

"We'll be here waiting for you, dears," she said, holding out her hand.

Dace held Agnes' hand in hers, again struck by her radiating warmth, and Beatt covered their clasped hands in his. All three watched as the spangled shards in Beatt's hands slid into Dace's. She gasped.

Dace withdrew her hand and held it up in the metallic light coming in the window of Agnes' office. The skin seemed to undulate like ocean shallows. Agnes raised her arm alongside Dace's. Her flesh remained solid.

Agnes patted Dace's arm. "You astound me," she said, smiling broadly, and rolled her chair back.

"See you for dinner?" Agnes asked, turning her head sideways to look at Dace and Beatt. "Plenty of leftover rice, vegetables, and apple crisp. If you need a snack, we're still working our way through a large donation of baby food we received several months before the convent was closed. You'll find the jars in the pantry."

At first Dace assumed Agnes was joking, but no punch line followed her straight-faced delivery.

"That was a difficult time. Moore Electric's offer hadn't yet materialized, but we had our faith—me, Elizabeth, and Miriam. We each took a vow of poverty before joining the order, so were accustomed to austerity, but we were all a bit despondent when the food was close to running out. Then we received the donation of baby food. The donor gave us so much, the delivery men had to bring the boxes in on a forklift. It felt like a miracle. When Moore Electric's offer came in a few months later, we were just tired enough of eating baby food at every meal to fully support it." She smiled. "That reminds me. Will you be back for dinner?"

"Yes," Dace said. She bent and gave Agnes a quick peck on her cheek, blinking away her tears as she did. Then she slid her hand into Beatt's, which felt like submerging it in water, and they left.

Dace turned out of the Station and eventually onto the main thoroughfare crowded with shops and restaurants. She approached a traffic light that blinked green to yellow. Dace braked and stopped as the light flicked to red. Murmurs arose on the sidewalk next to them.

"There's no one driving that car," someone called, and the pedestrians who had been about to cross the street gathered near Dace's car and peered in. "It's one of those driverless cars they're testing," shouted another.

Dace shrank away, overcome by claustrophobia. Beatt was

busy with the glovebox, repeatedly releasing the latch to pop it open and pushing it closed.

Someone rapped on the window on Beatt's side. He started.

"Hey, fella, what's it like?"

Beatt stared speechless at the face looming close to the glass.

The light turned green and Dace slowly pulled out, leaving behind the onlookers and their shocked faces. Her tight breathing lessened.

"That man looked like a Gigante," said a shaken Beatt.

"What do Gigante look like?"

"Tall, white, long, light hair."

Dace glanced in her rearview mirror. The fellow who had banged on Beatt's window watched them drive away. To Dace he looked like a rangy college student who played guitar in a covers rock band. *There had to be more to these Gigante than that*, she thought.

They stopped at her apartment to clean up and gather supplies. She showed Beatt how to turn on the shower. "More knobs," he commented, and she tucked her phone charger in her bag. She'd been off the grid for over twenty-four hours.

She gathered several outfits: two pairs of denim skinnies, one distressed and one dark denim for work plus a basic black blazer, long-sleeved, V-neck tops in black, gray, and dark navy, and two clean bras and several pairs of underwear, her everyday panties: lacy thongs.

After Beatt emerged from the bathroom in his borrowed clothes, which melded into his particle self, Dace took her turn. She stripped off her jeans, top, and bra and then, finally, the underwear she'd worn on her date with Ricci. The boy shorts gave off the faint scent of her body's musk, her shirt holding Ricci's sandalwood smell. *Ricci*, she called out in her mind. For a moment she felt him near her. Then she remembered that moment when he dashed off to help Jez. The sense of his presence faded. She lifted the lid of the rattan hamper. She tossed in her dirty laundry and secured the lid.

Dace drove to a strip mall between her house and Oblation Station. Under the fluorescent lights of the store, Beatt's form waved in vibrating strings, like beaded strands in a curtain.

"Try these," Dace said, handing a pair of dark blue denim jeans to Beatt.

As soon as the cloth touched his hands it too began to shimmer like heat waves on a hot highway. Dace laid her hand on his. Her flesh took on a glittery, diaphanous quality, with moving waves fluttering like the white fabric of Jez's Descenders' veils.

"Can I help you?" The young man walked slowly toward them with his hands jammed in the pockets of his trousers, worn belted but loose. He pushed his tortoiseshell spectacles up the bridge of his nose with his index finger. "Teetou, Trainee" his name tag read.

"We're looking for an outfit for my friend," Dace said.

He looked at Dace then dropped his gaze to her hand. He scanned the vision of her hand pressed over Beatt's and the pair of jeans. He raised his head and smiled, as he registered her eyes like a doctor flashing a pen of light during an examination. "Casual or formal?"

"They're for my friend," Dace said, gesturing to Beatt.

Beatt smiled which caused his pixelating self to glint in the harsh lighting. Motes of his shimmer traveled to Teetou, surrounding him like dust particles.

Teetou tilted his head back to peer at Beatt. "You can try them on, if you want, sir," Teetou said.

"You can see him?" Dace whispered.

"Pretty much." He tentatively stretched out his fingers

toward Beatt's vibrating form.

Beatt held out his hand. Teetou laid his palm over Beatt's. A faint glow swam up to the surface of Teetou's skin.

Teetou's shoulders hunched as he yelped with delight and he retracted his hand to cover his mouth.

Another clerk sporting a tag that read "Barry, MOD" appeared at Teetou's side.

"Everything okay?" he asked, with a smile for Dace and a narrow-eyed grimace for Teetou. "I'm the Manager on Duty, as you can see," he said, tapping his tag.

Dace nodded. "We're fine."

"Good to hear." Barry turned to Teetou and glared, punctuated with a menacing downward jab of his chin.

As Dace handed her credit card to pay for the two pairs of denim and two shirts, Teetou's pocket buzzed. He pulled out his phone, laying it on the counter near him, and glanced between it and the terminal where it processed the transaction.

"The north pole is wandering again," he said. "Earth's magnetic field is always changing." He laughed, a bark. "I have alerts set up for when it does." He glanced at his phone then, smiling, glanced back and forth between Dace and Beatt. His phone pinged again. He bent his head to it then looked up. "There's a scientist I follow who embeds microchips in insect larvae, and when the insects are grown, she harnesses the energy created by their wings to power the microchips. Cool, huh?"

Dace stared wordless at Teetou. Could he really be dropping a possible solution for Brandon's power source issue in her lap? She'd never experienced the universe so neatly presenting a missing puzzle piece, if that's what it was. Her mother always spoke of the cosmos working this way but, as with most of her other-worldly convictions, Dace had not believed her.

Beatt beside her tilted his head as he studied Teetou.

Barry appeared at Teetou's side. "No phones on the floor, Teetou, I warned you."

Teetou pocketed his device and handed the bags to Dace and Beatt. Barry snatched the bag he held out to Beatt. "Hand the bags to the guest, not to some invisible being beside her," he sputtered.

Teetou cocked his head. "The guest?" he echoed, then looked from Beatt's gauzy form to Dace. "Don't you mean guests? You know, plural, not singular?"

"Idiot," Barry muttered under his breath.

"Come with us," Beatt said so soft and low it sounded like a hum.

Beatt appeared not to see the warning message Dace telegraphed with her eyes.

Teetou opened his mouth to speak and the glowering Barry muttered, "Back to work," then sang out jovially to Dace and Beatt, "Have a nice day."

"Son of a Gigante," hissed Beatt as Dace whisked him away.

"What was that?" Barry exclaimed.

"He said, 'Son of a Gigante'," Teetou said and stepped out from behind the counter and trotted after Dace and Beatt.

"You're fired," shouted Barry as Dace hurried Beatt out the door, with Teetou following closely behind.

Chapter 15
The Invisible Goes to Work

TEETOU TALKED NON-STOP AS HE trailed Dace and Beatt to the front door of Oblation Station.

"I think we should be looking down, not up for an alternative energy source. Reversing the earth's poles manually just isn't an option. Believe me. I've done several thought experiments, and I got close but have concluded it just can't be done. But the insects; now there I think we have some possibilities."

"Teetou, can you give us a minute?" Dace asked.

"Sure," he said, and meandered away, coming to a stop inches from the thorns of the rose bushes. His chin dropped to his chest as he consulted his phone.

Dace drew in close to Beatt. "This is deeply weird," she said. "We leave to get you clothing and come back with a young man. I realize he's hinted at knowledge that might help solve a problem with technology Jez' brother is working on for my dad's company, but we don't know anything about him. Teetou sounds smart but is he stable? He just got fired. He must have people. They'll wonder where he is. Maybe he's mentally vulnerable. We don't know anything about him except he seems to perceive at least a couple of worlds."

Beatt's dark eyes shone.

Realization dawned. "Oh, okay, I get it. By nature or nurture, he isn't bound to the material world. But we can't just start collecting people with that ability. Let's introduce him to Agnes then I'll talk to him and at least get basic info and make any necessary phone calls."

"Come on, Teetou." Dace beckoned to the young man.

He trotted after them into the reception area where Dace introduced him to Elizabeth and Miriam behind the front desk who told them Agnes was in the kitchen.

As Dace and Beatt entered the kitchen, Teetou hung back in the darkness of the entryway.

Agnes was filling her thermos. She paused and looked up with a tilt of her head. A beaming smile stretched across her face. "Hello," she greeted them. "Will you come into the light?" Agnes asked Teetou.

Teetou stepped up to the center island where Agnes leaned into her walker.

"Teetou," she said, reading the name tag he still wore. "French?"

"Not French; American. My parents named me after a bandwidth connection."

The phone in his pants pocket sang its wail. He pulled it out and studied it. He looked up, seeking Agnes' eyes and instead finding the crown of her head. He dropped to the floor beneath her. He lay on his back at her feet so he could stare directly into her eyes, and she into his. He grinned. "The earth reversed its poles again," he said, holding up his phone.

"Teetou, how old are you?" Dace asked.

"Twenty-seven next month."

Agnes smiled down at Teetou. "There's a caretaker's closet

available for the next few nights. No chemicals in there, just the buckets and mops. It's not the Ritz, but a cot would fit and we have plenty of blankets. Would you like to stay here? Perhaps in exchange for some chores?"

Teetou smiled and nodded as his head rested on the linoleum floor.

Dace stepped forward. "Agnes, I—"

Elizabeth and a kitchen helper entered the room. They stepped carefully around Teetou and Agnes as they lifted pots from cupboards.

"Time to get up now, dear," Agnes said to Teetou.

Teetou rose from the floor and Agnes led him to the step outside the kitchen. She handed him a broom, and he began to sweep.

Agnes rocked back into the kitchen. Dace approached her and spoke in a low voice. "I think someone needs to vet Teetou."

Agnes' brows drew together in consternation.

"Sorry, corporate term. Vet means assess," Dace explained. "We need to know where he lives, if someone's expecting him, and whether he's someone who can make independent choices."

Agnes' brow remained furrowed. Beatt's shimmer was pricked with dots of charged light.

"We don't want the Station getting into any trouble by sheltering someone who might be under the care of someone else. I'll just talk with him, that's all, and make sure he phones anyone who might worry where he is."

At this Agnes' brow relaxed. "Of course, dear, you're right. I hadn't thought of that. You'll take care of it?"

"Yes." Accustomed to seeing her mother as child-like and adult at the same time, Dace easily took the same view of Agnes.

"Elizabeth," Agnes said, "will you orient Teetou, our newest helper, to the chores that need doing? He'll be staying with us for a few days, so we'll put a cot and blankets in the caretaker's closet for him."

"Of course," Elizabeth said, pausing in her stirring to turn toward Agnes. She tilted her head. "And where is this Teetou?"

"Out here," came Teetou's voice from the bottom step.

Elizabeth, along with everyone else, turned to see his dark head and jaunty wave. "It's a date," she said, waving back.

Agnes held her thermos to her heart as she rolled one-handed out of the kitchen. "I'll be in my study," she called back.

"Dace, we've moved you into a room on the oblates' wing to free up space on the retreatant side. We've put your name on the door. There are plenty to choose from, though; most of the Sisters left for other orders."

Elizabeth's inability to see Beatt hadn't resulted in a problem to solve, at least for the moment. Beatt could stay in any of the empty oblate rooms. Even so, a niggle of concern arose in Dace's mind: what would she do when the problem wasn't so easily taken care of? She tucked the thought in the back of her mind and addressed the more pressing issue.

"Teetou," Dace said from the doorway with Beatt behind her, "would you come with us and chat for a moment?"

"Us?" queried Elizabeth.

"Um, the royal we; old habit," Dace said quickly as she hustled a puzzled-looking Teetou out of the kitchen, Beatt's rippling form close behind.

Dace sequestered the three of them in the room where she had waited before her descent. She sat in the chair and Beatt settled his sparking form against the desk. Teetou plopped down on the cot.

"Will anyone be expecting you?" Dace asked.

Teetou shrugged and smiled cheerfully. "My parents won't exactly be expecting me but at some point they might wonder where I am. If they're not at work they're in their office at home. They're in IT security. Keeps them pretty busy."

"Could you call them and let you know where you are? And maybe let them know you're no longer employed, on the off chance they'd try to find you at the store?"

"Sure. But I should text them. They never answer their personal phones, and I'm not allowed to call their business number."

Teetou input a message. "Want to see it?" he asked, handing his phone to Dace.

"At Oblation Station with the nuns for a few days," read the text. "Got fired."

She was startled by the sharp, brief message and began to get a sense of how Teetou moved in the world. Like her mother, he had the freedom to live in two worlds, but unlike her seemed to have a slim connection to those in his immediate family. "I'm sure you know your parents better than I do." She handed his phone back to him.

He tapped his phone, and it emitted a whooshing. He pocketed it. "I'll forward you their message if they respond."

If, she thought. *Oh, dear.* "Won't they be concerned that you were fired?"

He shook his head. "They'll be glad. They won the bet, and now I have to go to work for them at their company." He let out a little yap of laughter. "Unless I stay here and become a nun."

Dace shook her head. "You'd be a monk, not a nun. And they're not nuns, they're oblates!" she finished, exasperated.

After turning Teetou over to Elizabeth, Dace led Beatt to the monastery dining room where Elizabeth and the helper had put out pans of baked macaroni and cheese and apple crisp.

"We should eat," she directed Beatt.

Each spooned steaming food on a plate, then sat at a table with their backs to the windows, giving them a view of the reception area.

Dace forked a small mound of macaroni and cheese, creamy with a chewy, browned crust, into her mouth. Two women in fluttering white veils had just arrived and spoke with Miriam who sat behind the front desk. Elizabeth and Teetou passed through on their way to straighten the retreatants' rooms. Teetou toted two plastic cleaning pails and a broom was wedged under his arm.

"I have to go to work tomorrow," Dace said.

Beatt shimmered like a mirage. "We," he corrected. "We go to work. I don't know what happens if I'm not near you, and I don't want to find out."

"Do you miss your home?"

"I was lonely there." He laid his fork on the table. But at least I knew I could find safety in the deeper level of Ssha Mountain. Before the Gigante I didn't worry about safety, and I never felt lonely. These are new things to me. So is being partially transformed in your world."

"What if you said 'enough'? Tap your ruby slippers together and go home?"

He cocked his head.

"Sorry, it seems I can't talk very long without using a figure of speech or cliché. Could you go back if you wanted?"

"What I want is also a new concept. That's just not how it's done in Ssha way. Who I am is woven into that way and the Ssha themselves."

"That sounds terrible. It's like you have no rights as a person. Like you're beholden to the Ssha. I'm so sorry." Dace placed her palm on his rough hand. He turned it and pressed his warm palm against hers and entwined his scaly fingers in hers.

She thought of holding Ricci's hand at Bahama Breeze and squirmed in discomfort. She tried to extract her hand from Beatt's grip but his warm fingers held her fast.

"There is joy, even exhilaration, in giving one's self over to a larger force," Beatt said. "That happens in sex, or so the hieros house women told me. That act served to transmit Ssha energy into the world. I know how to transmit it using my thoughts. What if you and I could transmit it the traditional way?"

Dace yanked her hand out of his grasp.

"Not here, of course," he continued.

Dace rubbed her hand.

"I'm sorry," he said.

They sat in silence for a few moments.

"This energy you refer to," Dace said. "We've developed a lot of ways to power the world. Maybe Ssha way isn't the only way?"

He glanced at the overhead lights. "Yes, I'm coming to understand that. But do any of these methods join the disparate parts inside humans?"

Dace shook her head. "Not so far. I'm afraid this new loneliness you've experienced is now pervasive, everywhere." She rejoined their hands. "Maybe we do need Ssha way."

~~~

From the reception area, Miriam's voice rose into a wail.

Dace leaned away from Beatt to get a better view of the atrium. A crowd of veiled woman swarmed through the front door and filled the reception area, hiding Miriam from view. In a few moments, Agnes rolled quickly into the atrium shortly followed by Elizabeth and Teetou. Then Jez and Peter flew in behind them.

"Let's try something," Dace said and rose and gestured for Beatt to follow her into the atrium.

"Descenders," Jez called out from where she stood off to the side of the reception desk, "welcome. We're thrilled you're here. Hashtag Jez for your social media posts! We'll get you checked in in a jiffy, just please be patient with us."

"Jez," Dace said loudly, waving her arm, "why don't you introduce staff and helpers so the Descenders will know who they can ask for help?"

Jez' face brightened. "Great idea! All staff and helpers, join me over here."

Agnes scooted in next to Jez, Teetou at her side. Elizabeth, Dace, and Beatt joined the line.

"Silence, my fellow descenders," Jez said in her resonant voice.

Quiet fell over the crowd except for Miriam's anxious murmurings and keyboard tapping as she checked in guests.

"To my left," Jez began, "we have the head oblate of Oblation Station, Agnes." Agnes bobbed her head. "Next to her we have—" Jez paused.

"Teetou," he supplied, grinning. "A helper."

Jez nodded. "Then we have Elizabeth, an oblate, and Dace—" she hesitated then said, "a helper."

The veiled women nodded, causing the gauzy cloth covering the bottom half of their faces to flutter. They looked expectantly at Jez.

"Say something," Dace whispered to Beatt. "Anything."

"I am Beatt," he said.

"What was that?" a woman in the front of the group said. She looked back and forth along the line of staff and then around the room.

"Sounded like one of those little relaxation fountains," said another descender.

"I am Beatt," he said again.

The descenders heads turned this way and that, looking

around the atrium. Jez frowned. Agnes tucked her chin more deeply into her chest, and Teetou looked quizzically at Beatt and Dace.

"Is the sound piped in?" one of the women said.

Jez shrugged and smiled. "We're still working out the kinks. Now why don't I bring name badges and a Sharpie around, and Peter can pass out the schedule for this weekend's descent."

Agnes nodded to Dace and Beatt, smiling broadly, and rolled out of the atrium. The buzzing of the women's voices rose, and Jez handed out the badges and markers.

"Teetou, back to tidying, shall we?" Elizabeth stood poised at one of the spokes of hallways.

"One moment, Elizabeth," he said and walked over to Beatt and Dace.

"Is your superpower invisibility?" he asked Beatt. "Wait," he said, briskly shaking his head, "that can't be right because I can see you. And Dace and Agnes can see you. In a sample of, say, forty humans, only three can see you. Those who can't see you can hear you but don't identify your sounds as speech. That's kind of a weird superpower. What were you thinking you'd do with it?"

"We haven't worked that out yet," Dace said, the impulse to both laugh and cry surging up in her.

Teetou nodded. "Okay, but let me know when you do. I can't wait to post about it."

Dace was horrified. "No, Teetou, you can't. It's… it's… an experiment, and we don't want to influence results by telling people."

"Oh, yeah, sure," he said, "my parents come up with crazy technology all the time and I'm sworn to secrecy until it's actually been tested and deployed. Which means I keep a lot of secrets." He laughed then sobered as he studied Beatt.

"You're kinda fading in and out."

"Teetou?" Elizabeth called out from where she stood next to a housekeeping cart stacked with towels.

"Gotta go," he said, and with a wave joined Elizabeth.

Dace and Beatt slipped out of the busy atrium. As they parted for the night in the quiet oblates' wing, Dace peered at him in the semi-darkness outside their rooms.

"I'm not sure I see what Teetou is talking about," she said.

Beatt held a hand up to his face. "I do. I noticed it. I'm afraid of what it means."

Again, she was wrapped in that claustrophobic sense of the material world closing in around her. "We'll talk to Agnes," she said, patting Beatt's shoulder, a sensation like placing her palm on slush.

Before closing her eyes for sleep later in her room, Dace plugged her phone charger in and connected her phone to the charger, but still did not turn it on.

The next morning, Dace dressed in an outfit that would pass muster for casual Friday--inky blue skinny jeans, black top, and black blazer. She had never broken the dress code. Others had, and their doing so had seemed to go unnoticed; they weren't sent home, weren't written up. She held her phone in her hand; she still hadn't powered it on. Doing so would be her official re-entry into what had been her usual world—Dad, Mom, her job. Meladee. Erupting in tears, she realized it would also be re-entry to the world that had opened up with Ricci then abruptly shut off to her. She didn't know if she could bear what might await her. Silence—no voice mails from Ricci—would be intolerable, but so would recordings of his voice.

As Dace and Beatt walked to her car, two vans pulled into the lot and disbursed two flocks of women wearing white half-veils. The women streamed up Oblation Station's steps and through the main doors into reception.

"Poor Miriam," Dace said. "Should we go back and help?"

Beatt shook his head, a flare of light and movement in the morning sun. "Even in my world, more business is a good thing."

Dace started the car and turned onto the main road leading to the highway and They Who Ride.

At Dace's office, Beatt hovered behind her as she stood at They Who Ride's main door, fumbling for her badge. Beatt wore his janitor's cap low over his see-through face. The cap, like all materials that came in contact with Beatt, winked with dancing shreds, devolving into the non-material.

Dace badged in, and Beatt slipped in behind her. Dace blinked in surprise. Instead of the usual dim light and the intense, focused vibe, as though the office were a submarine's radar room, the overhead lights were on, casting bright fluorescent light throughout the office. Paul and Charlotte in Finance chatted over their shared cube wall, laughed, then both sat down. The intern developers Nick and Sadie sat in the normally empty chairs in the reception area. Both worked on their laptops and engaged in a murmured conversation. Sadie suddenly punched the air with a victory fist. Then they both dipped their heads back to their machines.

Dace and Beatt passed Josh and Chad, both of whom nodded to Dace but did not acknowledge Beatt, nor did any of the other company's employees they passed. To Dace, this was potentially good news. It could be they couldn't see him though it could also be they were blinded by their joy in their new-found freedom.

Dace turned down the aisle to her cube. She slammed into Meladee who was in the aisle bent over in laughter.

"Why, it's Miss Dace!" Meladee crowed when she'd righted herself. Marjory across from her grinned and sat back down at her desk. "I was super mad at you until I got into work this morning and learned your dad, the boss of all of us, took a personal day." Meladee peered around Dace. She frowned. "That's a nice trick. Somebody playing with the projector?" She looked behind her then shrugged. "When the cat's away."

"You can see him?" Dace asked, alarmed.

"If by 'him' you mean a vaguely man-shaped sunbeam, yeah, mostly."

Marjory peered into the aisle, shrugged and went back to work.

Dace pulled Meladee by the arm back into her cube. "Mr. Banks took a personal day?"

Meladee nodded. "Yup," she said.

"He's never taken a day off. He didn't even take off the day I was born."

"Well, he did today, and he put Mark in Accounting in charge." She pointed over to a dark head a few rows away, and called, "Hey, Mark!"

Mark looked up from his machine and waved merrily.

"Told you," Meladee said. She flopped down in the chair in front of her docked laptop and slipped one earbud in her ear. The other dangled alongside her cheek like a strand of spaghetti. "Maybe he lost his mind with your disappearance."

Dace's eyes widened in horror.

"Just kidding," Meladee said. "He said in his email he had some pressing personal business to attend to."

It was catching, thought Dace.

"I could live with Mark's management style," Meladee noted. "It's sort of anti-management. I actually feel enthused about analyzing data. What a difference a little freedom makes. You're not off the hook, you know. Thank your dad for dispelling my fury at you. I can't believe how many texts and voicemails I left, and you didn't respond to any of them.

I was so worried about you."

"I'm so sorry," Dace said, whispering and bending down to lightly touch Meladee's forearm. Where she made contact, Meladee's skin gleamed and glistened. Meladee stared down at her forearm. "What the—" she began.

"I can't tell you everything now," Dace said in a hushed voice, rising back up. "Something extraordinary has happened. I'll tell you later at the testing tonight at Oblation Station."

She and the trick-of-the-light Beatt left Meladee staring at her forearm which still glowed.

While Dace powered up her laptop and logged in, Beatt edged behind Isaac, the day cleaning person, as he emptied the trash in the cube next to Dace's. Beatt pulled the duster out of Isaac's cleaning cart as he trundled it down the hall. The duster was made of sparkling, iridescent feathers. In Beatt's hands, they vibrated into a wave.

A meeting reminder for that morning's scrum popped up on Dace's laptop. She had ten minutes. Brandon strode past Dace, seeing neither her nor Beatt.

With Beatt trailing, Dace headed to the conference room.

Brandon sat at the table alone in the semi-darkness. Dace sat down next to Brandon, opened her folio, and opened a text document to begin scribing. Her eyes flicked up as Beatt stationed himself near the door.

Brandon glanced around the room then bent his head over his machine. "Come on, Dace," he muttered under his breath.

She cleared her throat.

Brandon looked up from his laptop. "How'd you do that?" he asked. "You weren't here a moment ago." He peered at her, his brow furrowed. "Are you cloaked?" Without waiting for an answer, he dipped his head back to his device. A few moments later he smiled and raised his head. "Jez got a call from a paranormal video producer, and they're talking about her own show."

Dace said nothing.

"She's trying to talk Jack into a position on the show. I think she's already got your mom, I mean, Mrs. Banks, roped into helping."

Dace's heart lurched at hearing Ricci's and then her mother's name in the same sentence as Jez's. Dace's childhood chant of the names of the invisible lines around the earth was not powerful enough to calm the wild rage that rose up in her. She stared at her folio and imagined steam coming out of her ears. Beatt shimmered over to her and lay his cool, barely visible hand on her shoulder. A layer of frost spread over Dace's heart. The out-of-control feelings quieted down. She let out the breath she'd been holding and resumed the scribe's position: head down, fingers poised over the keyboard. With a pat to Dace's shoulder that felt like soft rain, Beatt undulated back to his position near the door. He ran his duster around its frame, and its silky strands broke down into tiny speckles.

Dace's fingers flew nimbly as though playing an instrument to catch up with Brandon's words.

"You don't have to scribe everything I say." His face cracked into a smile. "Unless you find every word I utter especially brilliant."

She paused her fingers. "Sorry," she said, "habit. Mr. Banks said to capture everything you say. Just following orders."

"Weird that he's out today."

Dace would not be drawn into a casual discussion about Dad's behavior and remained silent. But her own thoughts churned. What could be enough to be her father's own personal DEFCON 1? Her eyebrows drew together in concern, and her emotions broadcast a signal. Beatt turned toward her and sent his own signal of concern back to her.

She looked up at his translucent face, wavering like the refraction of light through heat.

Brandon's phone pinged. He looked down then up, a toothy, ecstatic grin like a tear across his face. "The GEOV app is picking someone up."

Dace froze. Run, she thought, sending as panicked a signal as she could to Beatt. This only caused him to shimmy more quickly toward her.

"I've got the team's profiles in the app and the magnetometer installed on the camera at our test site." He paused to look up at Dace's unmoving fingers. "You should probably get this. The GEOV functionality is there, but we haven't actually tested it. The app has a small range right now, several yards." He touched his device. "It's got somebody. But I'm getting an error saying no match in the census databases going back 200 years." He sighed. "A bug. Better start an issue log."

Dace's shoulders sagged in relief as she started the log. Beatt flickered away from her.

Brandon jumped to his feet. "Dace, thought experiment. GEOV used by ghost hunters." Dace's fingers keyed.

Josh and Chad filed into the room. Meladee entered and sat near Dace. Beatt blinked. Meladee started as though she'd received an electrical charge.

Josh and Chad sat down across from Brandon.

Meladee swept her hand toward Beatt. When her hand encountered the glittery soup that was Beatt, her smile abruptly faded. She withdrew her hand and stared at it. She raised her head to look at Dace. "What the eff?" she mouthed.

Dace shook her head.

"Ready for me to start the meeting?" Brandon ran his hand over the hair at the crown of his head.

"This is just a check-in meeting for the testing session tonight," Josh said. "Do you have everything you need,

Brandon? We're testing GEOV's ability to create profiles for known and unknown entities, right?"

Brandon nodded. "Three knowns: me, Dace, and my sister Jez. The test system is on my company's servers so no security issues with the addition of a non-They Who Ride employee. Mr. Banks said he'll be there for the testing, and we can use him and Mrs. Banks as unknowns."

Dace looked at him in surprise while continuing to scribe.

He nodded to Josh and Chad. "I'll need you both onsite for troubleshooting."

"We're in," Josh said.

Brandon shrugged. "That's everything, then. I guess we're all set. If no one has anything for the scrum, we're done."

Josh and Chad left the room, murmuring back and forth in conversation. Only Meladee remained, glaring at the radiating shape of Beatt. Understanding dawned on her face, and she shot out of her chair and put her hands on her hips.

"Brandon, is this your way of showing off?"

Brandon looked uncomprehendingly at her.

"This... this hologram?" she asked, gesturing toward Beatt.

Brandon looked where Meladee pointed, and at first his gaze remained blank. Then he frowned and rose. He approached the wall behind Dace. Brandon scanned it up and down and side to side. Beatt faced Brandon full on. Both Beatt's and Dace's expressions grew frantic as he began dissolving. Brandon ran his hands through the air where Beatt stood, disturbing what looked like dust motes. His hands glinted. Then the vibrating column that was Beatt dimmed and went out. Dace's heart thudded with wild panic.

"It's part of the GEOV app but not part of the requirements so you can't say anything or Brandon will be in big trouble," Dace said in a rush.

Brandon turned and gaped at her.

"I knew it," burst out Meladee. "I'm definitely coming tonight. I want to see what else you've got cooked up. You, madam," she said, pointing at Dace. "We are way overdue for a debrief. Tonight, after the testing, no arguing."

She flounced out of the room.

Brandon shook his head at Dace. "I'm totally not following," he said.

"Thought experiment," Dace said. "You harness the kinetic energy of insect's wings. Find scientists who've implanted larvae with microchips and buy their robo insects. Their buzzing wings recharge the batteries built into their bodies. You no longer need to rely on external cells on the video cameras for power."

"Wow," Brandon said, moving away from where Beatt had stood and typed with one hand on his device and with the other gathered his things. "Man, this is good stuff."

A slow flicker grew next to Dace as Beatt resumed his partial form.

Dace shut her folio and left the conference room, with the glint that was Beatt close behind.

Chapter 16
The Redemption of the Dark

"I'M CONCERNED," AGNES SAID LATER that afternoon at the center. She sat with Beatt and Dace at a table in the empty dining room. Teetou sat next to Agnes. He pillowed his head with his bent arm, allowing him to see Agnes' face. "Brandon's nearness caused you to disappear, Beatt."

He gurgled.

"Your voice," Dace said. "I can't make out what you said."

Beatt nodded sadly. His outlines faintly pulsed.

"We no longer have the luxury of waiting," Agnes said.

Anxiety twisted in the pit of Dace's stomach.

Beatt rested his finger on her forearm, a wavering look of concern on his face. His touch brought Ricci's warmth and steadiness back into her thoughts which led to the memory of the sexiness in his solidity and unleashed restraint. The memory ignited responses in her body. Beatt's finger melded into her flesh creating a third substance, a heavy gel with pinpricks of electrical energy.

DOWN

Agnes tapped her spoon on the plate under the thermos cup. "We need to move more quickly, in order to master movement from the body-particle to wave-spirit."

An alert sounded on Teetou's phone. "Align the electromagnetic energy," he said. He stared off into the distance. "You could do that if you could control the energy by manually altering the earth's molten core. How to harness the shifts? If there's activity, there's kinesis. Turn the motion into more electricity while controlling the shifts. Reverse the planet's physics." He shook his head. "Too hard." A second alert blared. "Better yet, harness kinetic energy from insects' buzzing wings."

"Become the worm in the dirt," Agnes said.

Beatt gabbled, and Dace felt agreement in his sound though she could not make out the words.

"Seek darkness, not light," Elizabeth said, coming up behind them.

Four pairs of eyes shifted their gaze to her, three with solid irises, one with indentations filled with an opaque glow.

"Just wanted to let you know we are maxed out on retreatants for tonight's descent. Don't be alarmed if you see a multitude of women in white veils swarming to the descent cave." She took a breath and looked up, tapping her chin. "Oh, and before I forget, we've got quite a crowd coming this evening. Jez's potential producer is bringing a member of her film crew to scope out the center's grounds and descent area. Jez will give them the tour." Elizabeth consulted her clipboard. "Looks like the folks from They Who Ride will arrive at about the same time, seven p.m., for their testing, also in the basement."

"Maybe we should cancel testing," Dace remarked, hoping Agnes or Elizabeth would agree.

Elizabeth shook her head. "This is crowding we like, though

Miriam may disagree."

As though on cue, a yelp came from Miriam stationed behind the front desk.

Elizabeth glanced at the watch on her wrist. "Six-thirty, a bit early. So be it." She held up her hands with the fingers splayed into jazz hands. "It's showtime, folks!"

She dashed off to the reception area.

"Teetou," Agnes said, "will you help with traffic control? Direct people to available parking spaces?"

Teetou jumped up. "I'm on it," he said. He ran off, disappeared into the kitchen, then ran back in. "Forgot my phone." He picked it up from where it sat on the table, slipped it into his back pocket and charged back out.

Agnes turned to survey Beatt and Dace. "I do believe it's true that we need to act quickly. Beatt, do you feel you and Dace can merge this evening, instead of waiting for several more weeks?"

Beatt lay his other palm on Dace's forearm. Compliantly, her solid flesh swirled with jots of sparkle. He looked at Agnes and nodded.

"Dace?" Agnes asked. "Do you feel ready?"

Brandon's reedy treble filtered in from the reception area. Dace would have to endure the testing session—not attending would raise too much alarm and hub-bub—then she could move beyond it all and merge with Beatt in another place and time, as some other sort of being, one in between states of matter and particle. She would accomplish so much: keep Mom safe, which meant retaining her good daughter status with her father, even though she wouldn't be here to enjoy it. She felt a pang imagining life without Meladee's support, general dazzle, and a friendship that was surprising to Dace, who had few friends. *Who are you kidding*, she said to herself. *Meladee is your only friend.* But Dace was certain the loss of her in Meladee's life wouldn't crush her, not the way the loss of Jack Ricci had crushed Dace. She would do anything to forget the hurt and longing that still percolated within her.

"I do," Dace said.

Dace and Beatt rose, as did Agnes, pulling herself by the handles of her walker. Agnes extended her hand and Dace stepped forward to clasp it. She wanted to remember this, how it felt to have boundaries, be one being who could be touched by another, separate being. But she knew once she fully stepped into the void with Beatt, that memory along with everything else would dissolve.

"Agnes!" Miriam cried from the reception area.

"I'll help Miriam," said Agnes, releasing Dace's hand, and rolled out of the dining room. Dace and Beatt followed.

Miriam stood in front of the desk with her feet planted apart, as though to brace herself from the hordes. Her eyes behind her spectacles were wild.

Agnes joined Miriam. "How are we doing?" she asked.

"Oh!" Miriam said, throwing up her hands. "Chaos! Utter chaos. Brandon and his people just arrived and are on their way down to their testing room downstairs. Jez and the film crew are due any minute."

Dace and Beatt stood near the ring of windows which gave them a view of the entrance, the circular drive and the parking lot. Two cars, a van, and a compact with a ride-share placard on the passenger side window pulled in the drive. Teetou danced from foot to foot. He waved them toward him then directed them to turn into the gravel lot.

A woman with a green Army fatigue jacket and short, curly hair got out of the passenger side, and a young man in dark T-shirt and jeans and tan work boots the other. They went behind the van and a few minutes later emerged, the man carrying a camera that he hoisted on his shoulder. The woman consulted a notebook then looked around.

The paranormal show producer and the cameraman, thought Dace.

Jez emerged from the ride-share. As it departed, she shook her head full of long, dark hair so that its bounty swung around her shoulders. She wore large dark sunglasses, as though she were a celebrity traveling incognito.

"Jez Bell?" called the producer, Dace heard through an open window.

"Magritte?" Jez called back.

The woman nodded. Jez went to her and instead of shaking her outstretched hand pressed her palms together in front of her chest and bowed her head in Namaste.

A third car entered the drive, a dark green Lexus.

"Oh my God," Dace whispered to the luster that was Beatt, the last rays of the sun piercing him. "My parents."

Teetou swung his arms in a circle like a traffic cop, directing them into the lot.

Her parents parked and got out of the car. Dad stood ramrod straight outside the car and bent his head to his phone. Mom joined him. She stood in the twilight hugging herself. She looked around as though searching. Her eyes lighted on Jez. She leaned toward her husband. She spoke to him, nodding toward Jez. He kept his head bowed over his phone. Mom again spoke to him, her head tilting as though asking a question. He shook his head and placed his phone back in his pocket.

As her parents joined Jez, Magritte, and the cameraman, a third vehicle pulled into the circular drive: a white Tahoe. Dace's knees buckled and she held the window frame for support. Teetou directed the driver into the last space in the lot. Jack Ricci got out of the car. He was in his usual uniform, a black business suit. The stiff collar of his white shirt was buttoned at his neck, and a blood-red tie hung down his front. His eyes were dark, his expression inaccessible. Like Mom, he cast a probing gaze around the grounds. Jez spotted him. She started at a run across the gravel then tipped awkwardly on the uneven surface. She careened toward Ricci, who stepped back, and Jez fell into him, throwing her arms around him. To steady himself, he gripped her waist, in a hold Dace knew so well from just their one short evening together. Her solar plexus retracted, and she curled in on herself as though someone had landed a punch to her gut.

Ricci peeled Jez's arms off as though they were a squid's tentacles. She grabbed his hand and pulled him toward Dace's parents and the woman and the man, but he snatched it out of her grasp. Jez swept her arms up, down, and to the sides as she performed the introductions like a wizard who had brought these disparate people together. Dad and Ricci nodded at each other, though Dad held the gaze a beat too long, as though Morse coding him a message with his eyes. Mom seemed ecstatic to meet the producer and the cameraman. When Jez introduced Mom to Ricci, she briefly covered her mouth with her hands, as though to hide her wide smile, then dropped them and bobbed her head to him with her hands folded in Namaste against her chest.

Dace felt like the little girl in the horror story from Night Gallery, who the life-size doll had tricked into changing places. Whatever position Dace had once had with her parents and Jack Ricci, Jez Bell now seemed to occupy. Dace's place was now the doll's box. The group made their way to the front steps of the center. Ricci continued his appraisal of the center, looking down, up, and at both sides. Mom, in less robotic fashion, did the same. Dad lightly held her elbow. Dace felt rooted to her spot, a sentinel at the window.

Agnes joined them at the ring of windows, her gaze, as

usual, at the floor. She swiveled her head up sideways to watch the small crowd coming up the steps. She placed her warm palm on Dace's forearm. "Everyone will be inside momentarily. Are you comfortable confronting them?"

Beatt laid his forearm along Dace's. Her flesh quickly melted into his in a swirl of glittering specks. The sensation of becoming more particle and less matter put great amounts of space between her feelings and thoughts. The ache of Ricci not choosing her downgraded to a twinge as its electrical intensity reduced, like turning down the dimmer switch. The blow she'd felt in her very center as Jez had embraced Ricci broke up like a signal that was only partially getting through, then died down to a mere blip.

Dace patted Agnes' hand then gave it a squeeze, as much as she could with her lava-lamp flesh. She nodded. "We'll go now," Dace said, releasing Agnes' hand. "Come on, Beatt, let's get downstairs to Brandon's testing, then as soon as we can, we'll... do whatever we have to do."

As the front door creaked open, together Dace and Beatt sped down the hall. A jelly fish-like glow emitted from underneath her skin. Beatt blew like smoke beside her. Dace drew abruptly to a stop at the elevator and aimed her index finger at the "B" button. Dace's finger pressed into it as though it were bread dough. She extracted her finger, and the elevator dinged.

They took the elevator to the basement, and Dace led Beatt down the dark hall to Brandon's designated testing area.

She crept up to the open doorway, both she and Beatt hanging back in the dark hall. They both softly glowed.

"Everyone got their devices on?" Brandon asked.

Josh and Chad waved their phones at Brandon in a "Yes," and Meladee glanced down then up and nodded.

Dace edged into the room. Beatt hovered just outside.

"Dace?" Meladee studied her, tilting her head this way and that trying to make her out. "Dace!" she then exclaimed and ran over to her.

"Back where you were, please," Brandon directed Meladee, his gaze still on his phone, Josh and Chad likewise. "Dace," Brandon said, without looking up, "looks like your phone isn't on. Power up, please."

Reluctantly, Dace pulled her phone from her bag. As she pressed the power button, which gave way like the elevator button, she avoided Meladee's piercing stare by concentrating on her LCD.

"Can Dace stand with me?" Meladee asked. She trotted over to Dace and pulled on her arm. She suppressed a squeak as her fingers sunk into Dace's arm. "What's going on?" she whispered. "Did Brandon turn you into a hologram? I'll kill him if he did."

"No, I want Dace back where she was, by the doorway," Brandon said in answer to Meladee's question.

Meladee reluctantly released her hold on Dace's arm. She stared at her hands as they seemed to come loose from something soft and malleable. She stepped backwards, her eyes never leaving Dace, until she had resumed her original spot.

Dace's phone beeped as it fully powered on.

"Okay, Dace, got you," said Brandon. "Next I need the unknowns to...." He studied his phone. "Damn, I thought I fixed that bug."

"What is it?" Josh asked.

"I'm registering someone who doesn't have a corresponding entry in the birth databases. He or she has a heartbeat but man, it's practically reptilian, like, ten beats per minute. Could I have debugged the bug and made it worse instead of fixing it? Oh my effing God," he exploded, smacking his forehead. "Now it shows not just one of whatever this is but multiples, like a bunch of dead reptilian ghosts. Josh, Chad, huddle."

The three gathered around a waist-high shelf where each had placed his open laptop.

As they worked, Meladee's face scrunched into confusion as she scrutinized Dace.

"Now," whispered Beatt behind Dace, in a voice like steam.

Beatt came to stand behind Dace and fully up against her body. Strands of himself wrapped around and throughout her. She felt prickles. Her form wavered. She looked down at her glittering self then back up at Meladee. Meladee's jaw hung open in shock.

A commotion sounded in the hall outside the testing room. Jack Ricci appeared in the doorway, Dace's parents behind him.

Ricci reached to grab Dace but his hands moved through her as though she were made of air. She felt the tickle of Ricci's fingers but Beatt's vibration had grabbed and rocked her with small movements that existed in this world and perhaps in another. Beatt extended his wavy strands toward Ricci and encircled him. Ricci's eyes grew wide as his physical form lost definition. The air within the energetic triangle that she, Ricci and Beatt formed smelled of limestone and wet rocks. She couldn't let Ricci accompany her. Dace gathered Beatt's strands in both hands and pulled hard. Released, Ricci hardened into flesh, blood, and bone. She wrapped Beatt's tentacles fully around her. Her bag and inside it her phone took on her diaphanous quality.

Ricci extended his outstretched arms toward her as she melted into Beatt. Her ability to see was fading, but she saw her parents, horrified, behind Ricci and Ricci's eyes, green, charged and steely.

DOWN

As though they were ectoplasm, Beatt floated their joined being up from the floor. Rapidly losing his material being, and Dace hers, Beatt, with Dace melting into him, shot up and through the ceiling, the two by four planks between floors, then the wood floor. He and Dace, or what was left of both of them, hovered above the kitchen floor. The room was dark, but Dace's eyesight was fading. She shut her eyes and could still make out the shadowy outlines of the kitchen. She kept her eyes closed as Beatt maneuvered them out the back door and down the steps, as though he were a force behind a wave, and lowered them so they hovered above a patch of dirt.

Agnes appeared in the doorway with Teetou at her side as Beatt, interwoven with Dace, hovered above the dirt.

Beatt pressed what was left of him into her, and several inches of his corporeal body, sparkling, slid deeply into hers. It felt like a piercing of each individual pocket of life in her body. Beatt poured into her. His cells slid into hers, hers slid into his, and both began to liquefy into particles.

A covey of women in their white birdcage veils exploded behind Agnes. Agnes thumped down one step, and the veiled descenders surrounded Agnes, assisting her down the remaining steps.

Agnes edged in her walker toward the column of sparkling smoke that was Beatt and Dace, and the swarm of women enclosed them like butterflies.

Agnes reached through the veils into the air over the dirt and into another dimension. She felt for whatever was left of Dace and Beatt. Through the softness of the veils, her hand encountered Dace's arm transforming from flesh into liquid.

The warmth of Agnes' touch momentarily called Dace back into particle. She held herself there, pressed against Agnes' hand, while Beatt worked, it seemed, to complete the final shift. She saw in her mind a stone wall with a hollow big enough carved in it big enough for two people. *Will I become stone? Or just lay on a stone bed?* thought Dace. Jack Ricci's face then appeared in her mind. Her heart squeezed. Or did Beatt's? His form had melted into hers, and he held her tightly in that merged embrace. *Agnes,* she implored, channeling thought from her watery self to Agnes' retreating hand.

In a moment of panic, Dace cried out in her mind to Agnes, "No, I don't want to."

Elizabeth appeared at the top of the steps. "Descenders," she shouted. "Not here! Wrong location. Follow me!"

The women in their white veils banked like a murmuration of birds and flowed across the dirt toward Elizabeth gesturing from the doorway. She led them away. Their buzzing faded, and silence fell.

Agnes rolled away then heaved herself and her walker up a step. Teetou helped her mount the remaining two. With Teetou protectively behind her, Agnes wheeled into the kitchen.

Dace dropped away from Agnes' hand. In moments she would be fully transformed from particle into wave, ready to traverse space and time.

Help, she called out in her mind.

A bangled wrist shot toward her. The hand groped, and Dace willed her hand to extract itself from the joined being she'd become with Beatt, but she could not. The hand withdrew.

Mom, Dad, Dace called out silently in her last few remaining moments of earthly consciousness.

Two hands, one pale, one burnished, materialized in what was left of Dace's sight. Again, Dace willed her own hand back into flesh to clasp this lifeline but she was too far gone in the transformation. The pale hand too began to dissolve and the burnished hand pulled it away.

Ricci, Dace called out in her mind, now nearly as vast as the universe, *Jack Ricci*.

A hand with sparse black hairs plunged in and grasped Dace's hand. At Ricci's touch, her flesh crystallized back into form. He held her hand tightly, and with mighty strength, he pulled her out of the wave energy field.

They fell back against the hard ground. Ricci protected Dace with his body, armored in his black business suit, wrapping his arms around her and holding her tightly to him.

Ricci sat them both up, never loosening his hold. Her parents stood behind them, with Meladee at their side. Her father opened his mouth to speak. Footsteps thundered down the back steps. Dace turned in Ricci's arms. Magritte and the cameraman stood at the bottom of the steps, Jez and Peter behind them.

"Quick, get that thing dissolving," Magritte shouted.

The cameraman pointed his camera to the column of mica that was Beatt. Magritte stood behind the cameraman.

Jez flew at what was left of Beatt. She held her phone in one of her outstretched hands as though she were jumping into a pool.

"Jez, no," croaked Dace.

Jez leaped into the sparkling vortex. Everyone but Ricci gasped.

Dace's father held Mom tightly as though she might fly out of his arms.

"You're getting this, right?" Magritte shouted.

"Yeah, yeah," the cameraman said.

They all watched silently as the light grew dim then went out altogether.

"My God," Magritte breathed. "Did we really just see that?

Jez actually going into the void?"

Then there was a pop, and Jez was jettisoned out from wherever she'd disappeared and landed with a thump on her ample bottom on the hard ground.

Magritte barked at the cameraman, "Get this."

The cameraman walked toward Jez, crouching to keep the angle in line with her face.

Dace briefly buried her face in Ricci's shoulder to muffle her laugh, as raspy as a frog's croak. Meladee clapped her hand over her mouth as she burst into laughter. Dace's mother covered her eyes. Dad and Ricci remained still, unflappable, but their grips on the women in their respective arms gave lie to their calm.

Jez' face scrunched up in fury. She rose from the ground and stood there fuming with her fists clenched. Peter tripped down the steps and ran to her side. He put a protective arm around her, and she swatted it away. She opened her mouth to speak, then, as all of them stared at her, she snapped her mouth shut. She hauled herself to her feet, grabbed Peter's arm and stomped away with him in tow.

"Where's my phone?" was the last thing they heard Jez shout.

Together, Magritte and the cameraman followed Jez and Peter who had reached the parking lot.

"Jez, wait, I think we can salvage this," Magritte called.

Jez turned and waited with her hands on her hips.

Ricci slowly got to his feet and helped Dace rise with him. They turned to face Meladee and her parents.

Meladee's phone made a trilling sound like evening crickets. She glanced quickly at it then back up at Dace. "Brandon says it's an emergency, and I need to get back down to the testing room. You owe me a tell-all," Meladee said, swooping in to quickly kiss Dace's cheek. "But later, when you're back to full power." Her glance flicked to Ricci then back to Dace. "I'm just glad you're okay." With a nod to Ricci and Dace's parents, Meladee dashed up the kitchen steps and disappeared into its darkness.

"I'm with Meladee," Mom said. "You owe us a tell-all."

"When I get my words back," Dace rasped.

Dace's mother took her hands in hers. She smiled. "I was right after all," she said. "True love does conquer all."

Mom turned back to Dad. He stared blankly at her. "Honey? Are you okay?" She pulled him close to her and searched his face. "Connor?" He remained mute and motionless.

"Guess I'd better get Dad home. Maybe the shock of me being right is too much for him," she joked. Dad's face was expressionless. Mom looped her arm through his. "Dace, we'll talk to you tomorrow. You're in good hands." She nodded at Ricci. She turned Dad and they headed toward the parking lot.

"Mom, wait," Dace called in a hoarse voice. Mom turned. "Who was the Devil card for in the tarot reading you did when I came by before the descent?"

"Both of us. The Devil stirs up trouble for his own ends. I didn't realize the card was for both until this morning. We'll talk more tomorrow." She resumed guiding Dad to the parking lot.

"I hope Dad's okay."

"Shock, I think, at what all saw. Or thought we saw. It will wear off." He took both of her hands in his, like he had at Banana Breeze. He tilted his head and kissed her, a long, firm, sweet kiss.

"I thought I was gone forever," she said and buried her face in his neck, his stiff shirt collar pleasantly scratching against her cheek. "How did you find me?"

"We had your profile in GEOV. Brandon had a breakthrough after he'd been playing with something in the app in a different testing environment. In this sandbox system, he'd programmed the GIS software to reach coordinates below the earth's surface. He switched over to that when he was working on the bug with Josh and Chad to see if that would make a difference. As soon as you turned on your phone, there you were in this other version of GEOV. Brandon didn't realize his programming the GIS software to reach below the earth's surface was actually tracking you after you and that... thing... began changing structurally. Brandon thought it was a bug."

"He's not a thing," Dace said. "He helped me not go insane when I thought I'd lost you. And his name is Beatt."

"Wherever he took you, whatever realm you were in, the alternate GEOV test app found you."

"Does that mean you can track Beatt?"

"I wish I could," Ricci said, brushing her hair off her brow. "I'd find him and do unkind things to him."

"But he's not a bad guy."

"He almost took you away, so in my book that makes him a bad guy." Ricci hugged her, aligning his body to hers. "I didn't tell Brandon his sandbox version was actually working. Only you and I know about it. I'd prefer it stay that way."

Dace pressed against his warm, muscled body. "We can argue later," she said. "When I get my words back."

Ricci leaned back and cupped her face in his hands. "I've never minded fewer words. I don't have that many myself." He kissed her. "Those I have are probably enough for both of us, until you get yours back. All that matters is that you're here now, with me; I'm not going anywhere, and I'm definitely not letting you out of my sight again."

He kissed her again, longer, with a pressing intensity. "Let's go," he said.

The kitchen door creaked on his hinges. They both turned.

"Dace, please, may I speak with you?" Agnes stood at the top of the stairs, her head hanging low over her walker. Teetou stood behind her.

Dace shrank away. Ricci tightened his hold. "You can speak to us," he said.

"I'm so sorry," Agnes said in a voice full of anguish. Teetou placed his hand on her curved back. "I went too far. I got carried away with what I thought was the mission. I panicked when I realized we were so close, and Beatt was unable to hold his form here in our dimension."

Dace turned in Ricci's protective hold to look up at him to gauge his reception of this information. He looked steadily, neutrally at Agnes, revealing nothing in his eyes or his gaze.

"Can you forgive me?" Agnes asked. She sagged on her walker.

"I'm going to help you in now, Agnes," Teetou said.

As Teetou helped Agnes maneuver the walker around, Dace wheezed, "I do. I do forgive you."

With a final wave to Dace and Ricci, Teetou closed the kitchen door behind them.

"Now we're going," Ricci said.

Dace lay her head in the crook of his neck and let Ricci guide her to the parking lot and his white Tahoe. Once inside, her eyelids drooped heavily, and she slept on the short drive to her apartment.

Later, after again she'd taken Ricci into her arms and they lay in her bed, Ricci deeply asleep, Dace's phone buzzed twice in quick succession. She lifted it from the bedside table. She had two texts, one from Meladee and one from Brandon.

We're at Banana Breeze, read Meladee's text. Brandon is clueless. He's cuter that way. You do know eventually you gotta tell me all?

Dace texted a heart.

Brandon's text included a screenshot: latitude and longitude in geographic mapping showing a location deep within the earth. The new layers via Brandon's new API showed crystalline caves, on the eastern coast of Crete, where a watery form lay immersed in a pool of green water, near slumbering giant reptiles, beings with in-laid pearls in their jaws and held in stasis in translucent beds.

Brandon sent a second text: Just lost the image in the app! Glad I grabbed it. It was there, then a beat later it was gone. Crap. More bugs for the issue log.

Beatt didn't make it, thought Dace. *His heart must have stopped and that's why he no longer registered in the app.* Her own heart grew heavy with sadness.

Ricci slept on his side and snored lightly. Dace pulled the blanket up over both of them, lay back, and faced him. She wanted to stare all night, drinking him in, and rejoiced that she could do exactly that if she wanted to. She caressed his cheek.

He woke.

"Sorry," she whispered. "Go back to sleep."

"Is everything okay?"

In the darkness she weighed telling him versus not. Arriving at the answer was easy and quick: she could not share her grief around what had happened to Beatt, how he had paid for participating in what he thought was for the greater good with his life. She knew if she even mentioned Beatt's name Ricci would fly into defense mode.

"Everything's fine." She was surprised by the lie and how easily it slipped out. *Is it a lie if it keeps the peace?*

His eyes closed and he slept.

This is love, she thought as she drifted off, content with minor duality if she could live like this forever.

Coming Soon...

RETURN OF THE GODDESS
Book III of the No Boundaries Trilogy

Read on for a preview of Chapter One!

Return of the Goddess
Chapter One

SIX-THIRTY A.M. ON A SEPTEMBER Norfolk morning, and the sun was bent on smoking anything and anyone in its path, including the women gathered in the commuter lot adjacent to the Norfolk Naval Air Station wearing pieces of cloth that covered their noses and mouths. But the women endured. They raised their placards stapled to wooden stakes. They stabbed their signs at the sky and the sun and chanted: "The goddess has returned!" and "Your seven thousand years are up!"

Dace idled in one of the slow-moving lanes of traffic at the gated entrance to the Naval Air Station. Her head turned to the women, she recognized Amelia, one of Jez' descenders, from that night at Oblation Station. Dace shrunk down behind the tinted glass of her car window. *Come on, come on*, she silently implored the lines of cars to move more quickly through the base's security kiosks.

"Will you look at that," Mom said, pointing at the sky above the veiled women as she peered out the windshield of Dace's car. "A horned moon. They're rare in our part of the world." She shook her head in wonderment. "It's my first sighting."

Dace glanced at the sky in the direction of Mom's finger. She squinted. Yes, she could see that the faint smear of white was the quarter moon lying on its back, its opposite ends curving up like the Cheshire Cat's smile. However, she pretended she couldn't, an old habit recently resurrected. "Looks more like a scythe or a simitar."

Mom shook her head again. She had many varieties of nuanced head shaking these days. "You and your dad. Do you realize how many times I've had to listen to you two do that over the years? Deny what I say I saw? And now you both experience something that proves the existence of the worlds I've been telling you about, and even that's not enough to change your minds. Though why he went mental, drained of his identity, and you didn't beats me."

Dace's hunching down allowed Rowena room to see out the driver's side window. "Oh, look!" she exclaimed. "There's Amelia, one of Jez' original descenders. Looks like she's leading the chants. She was there that night at Oblation Station when Beatt sucked you into his vortex and Jack Ricci rescued you. I call her 'the hair,' but only to myself. I used to have long, big beautiful hair that like. But you know that." She touched Dace's shoulder. "Let's yell 'hey'. I'll bet she'd love to meet you, the one who got this whole thing going for Jez, her streaming show and all." Mom reached across Dace, aiming for the button to lower the window.

The car in front of them inched ahead.

"Can't," Dace said, gently moving her mother's arm back to own space. "Sorry, but I've got to pay attention here."

Dace shifted the car quickly into Drive to move out of the line of sight between them and the women.

Her mother sat back in her seat.

Mom's mute seething came at Dace in shards of filaments that stung when they pierced her heart. *Shades of Beatt*, she thought.

In the past, when Dace or Dad kindly said, "No," to any suggestion they move, even briefly, into Mom's world, she fluttered her hands and giggled and said, "Oh, you two." Now she became silent.

The fan for the car's air conditioning faltered, the airy hum dropping to a sputtering wheeze. Mom flapped the edges of her cotton wrap skirt, homemade out of fabric covered in pink and orange flowers and looked back out at the women.

"I wonder if they're using the sign I made," she said. "It was a good one. 'The goddess has returned, don your veil' in dripping red letters. You know, like menstrual blood?"

Dace flipped the air conditioning off and after a few moments turned it back on. "I need to listen to the fan."

To Mom's raised brow, Dace responded, "That's what the mechanic told me to do when it does this. She said it'll tell her more about what's going on." Again, Dace turned off the AC.

Mom flapped more furiously. "I can't believe it's been only two weeks." She lowered the window and let in the hot air. "My, how time's fun when you're having flies!" she said. "That's Kermit the Frog, you know. Though in our case we're not having flies, we're having...." She paused. "You're having a romance with the human who saved you from an otherworldly being, your dad's having a breakdown, and I don't know what I'm having. Not fun, that's for sure."

Dace turned the air conditioning back on. She held her ear to the vent while keeping an eye on the car in front of them. She and Mom were next. "Focusing, Mom."

Shadowy shapes moved behind the dark glass of the guard's kiosk. A khaki-clad arm extended and gloved fingers reached toward the other car driver's offered piece of identification, a driver's license, Dace supposed. After a moment khaki arm held out a stiff rectangle which the fingers of the civilian took. Khaki arm disappeared into the gloam of the kiosk. The gate rose, and the vehicle drove onto the base.

Dace inched the car forward, and the veiled women left her peripheral perception entirely.

Inside the Military Police's kiosk two shapes moved behind the dark glass. The side door opened and a an M.P. in a white helmet and white bands across his khaki uniform stepped out, and Dace lowered the window. The singeing heat smacked Dace like a storm front.

Rowena leaned across Dace and extended a license plate toward the M.P. who reflexively jumped back. His partner in the shadows of the kiosk sidled alongside him and assumed a defensive stance, the weight in his pelvic region a ballast against unknown incoming.

Rowena leaned her full weight into Dace's side, her heavy, wavy hair enveloping Dace's face with its scent of hot hair and coconut oil, and propped the license plate up in the seam of rubber that ran flush with the lowered window of the car door. "See?" She tapped the red square in the bottom left corner. "We have a base sticker, just not the car that goes along with it."

The M.P. gingerly took the pressed metal plate from her. "One moment, ma'am," he said, and he and his cohort disappeared into the kiosk.

"Okay, Mom, you can sit back now," Dace said from inside the hot cloud of her mother's hair.

She laughed. "Sorry, forgot where I was for a moment."

"Oh, Mom," muttered Dace, an old refrain from a life spent with her mother and her beliefs in shifting, multiple realities and entities from other realms. Now Dace could use the same utterance with her father as he tried to recover from the ontological shock of experiencing first-hand the reality of her mother's beliefs by watching Beatt, half-man, half-lizard, metamorphose into whirling particle and attempt to take Dace with him. All he knew himself to be fell away after that night. He struggled to regain a sense of his old self or develop a new one. One morning two months into his medical leave he decided to jump-start himself by going back into work. He backed out of the driveway and onto their quiet Virginia Beach neighborhood road, put the car into drive, and accelerated smoothly down the street. Their next-door neighbor pulled out after him and waved as he passed Rowena, who waved cheerily back, then headed down the street in the same direction as Dad. Dace, watching from the porch, jumped when the metallic bang and crunch followed a few moments later, and ran to catch up with Rowena who sped down the street toward the noise.

The M.P. appeared. "Sorry, ma'am, you're clear. You can't display this on your dash," he said, handing the license plate to Rowena who handed it to Mom. "This you can." He handed Dace a visitor's pass placard which she placed on the driver's side dash.

The M.P. nodded crisply and raised the metal arm to allow them to pass through onto base property.

Dace wound through the base streets, Mom issuing directions she read from a slip of paper.

Neither Dace's car's GPS or her phone would work on base, though she knew the visitor placard sitting innocently on her dash held a tracking chip.

"Make your next right," Mom said, "and I'll start looking

for numbers on the building. There." She pointed to a building on the left. "Eleven Thirteen A."

A figure flitted in Dace's peripheral vision. *Crap*, she thought. *Begone, you other-worldly entities.*

Dace had become a beacon for transforming beings ever since her time with Beatt. She'd always been on their radar—various beings had blipped in and out all of her life—but spending time with Beatt had increased her signal.

The figure persisted. It emerged from her side vision and took the shape of a strong, husky man with a full head of dark hair, and for a moment it seemed Jack Ricci was coming toward her, arms outstretched, the same arms that pulled her from the clutches of Beatt's scaled arms as together they devolved into particle. Dace had stayed in those arms throughout the night before and after powerful, body- and mind-shattering sex. Ricci pounded her back into her physical self. There was just enough adrenalin rush to fuel Dace's recounting the entire story of Beatt, what he really was and her part in Sister Agnes' plan to allow him to metamorphose into their realm. "I'll never let him get near you again," Ricci murmured and fell asleep.

The next morning, when he was fully dressed and drank coffee with Dace at her small kitchen table, he again promised he would do whatever it took to protect her from Beatt, or "that thing," as he called him. She explained he had gotten it wrong; there was no longer a Beatt in their time; he had dissolved into the non-physical and was likely back in his own, ancient time in a cave on what now was Crete. Along with the slumbering giant reptiles or the Ssha, who had invented the Goddess to serve as their representative. All Ricci said to this was, "Never mention me and 'wrong' in a sentence together. I said I would keep you safe from him, and I will." Then he took her in his arms, crushing her against him, and buried his face in her long, curly hair then kissed her. He drew back. "And I mean that I will protect you forever." Dace climbed fully onto his lap, straddling him, and let him pull open her robe as she unbuckled his belt. "Can't," he whispered. "Got to catch my flight. Soon."

While her father went into a kind of catatonia, Ricci went to work. He had accepted a government engineering contract job that took him away to Nebraska which to Dace meant grain fields and cattle. He called her at unexpected intervals during the two weeks he had been away and promised a visit soon and ending every call with the same question: had she heard from that thing?

Dace realized he would never—could never—believe what Dace had told him: Beatt was a half-man, half-lizard who had metamorphosed here with the help of Sister Agnes at Oblation Station and Dace. Almost metamorphosed.

If Ricci gone somewhere slightly more exotic, say, Dubai, her explanation could satisfy Mom—Dad didn't ask, too busy drifting around their house like a shade—and her friend Meladee when they asked about him. Nebraska did not satisfy.

Dace was held in place by the sight of shape now wavering unsteadily, like heat waves on a hot road. Rowena's gaze followed hers and she cocked her head to the side. "I don't see it, but I feel it," she said. "Best to not engage. We don't want another Beatt on our hands!" she said, laughing. "That would just about finish your dad off, wouldn't it?"

True, thought Dace. But she didn't want to consider it. Mom's once-laughable store of knowledge about the other-worldly was now the new reality. This was not the outcome Dace could have imagined with the return of the Goddess. Her mother was her only lifeline to understanding the weird world she had unleashed with Beatt, and she still struggled to take it in. A lifetime of brushing off her mother's views was an old habit. It was a near-robotic reaction, and it clashed Dace's desperate neediness to understand this new world she inhabited. Anger was easier.

"Dad's condition doesn't seem funny to me," Dace said, unbuckling her seat belt. "Dad broke down after learning what he thought was a world of fantasy is in fact the truth, rendering his beliefs as lies."

Mom patted her hand, "I know, honey. I'm sorry learning that I was right was so shocking to your dad that he couldn't leave the couch in his den for two months. Who wouldn't be depressed to realize all he thought was real was not all this time his loving wife who could only hold part-time retail jobs understood the true nature of reality? And then when he finally pulls himself off his pity pot, he can't drive two blocks without getting in an accident. He said he didn't see the stop sign. This from a man who once out-maneuvered enemy fighter jets."

"Mom, please, stop," said Dace, pressing her forehead against the steering wheel.

"You think he'd ask me, 'How did you know? Teach me how you knew. I am ready to receive your knowledge!' But no, he sulks. And sulks."

Dace sat back against the seat. "The psychiatrist says cognitive dissonance can immobilize a person, even cause depression. Doesn't that worry you?"

Rowena rolled her eyes. "What about having your beliefs

mocked for years? Don't I get sympathy for that?"

If Rowena had been anyone else, Dace would have supported her indignation. But she was her mother, her slightly spacey mother who seemed to so easily tolerate skepticism from others, including her husband and daughter. It had never occurred to Dace this was learned, a skill that took teeth-grinding years to become habit.

"Are you and dad splitting up?"

"I don't know. It's not a fun household these days."

Rowena turned toward Dace. "What does Jack say about how the experience affected him?"

"He doesn't. He ran away, and when he calls all he can talk about is how he'll mess up 'the thing,' as he calls Beatt, if he ever comes near me again. Ricci doesn't seem to realize 'that thing' is no longer in our reality."

"Denial," Mom said, slapping the seat. "Same as your dad, just a different form. Goddamnit!" she shouted. "The Goddess returns and everyone's too absorbed in themselves to notice. That damn Jezebel. She's turned it into a freak show for her financial benefit."

Exhausted, she flopped back against the seat. Tears ran down her cheeks.

Dace lightly touched her shoulder. "Should we do this another day?"

Rowena shook her head and dabbed at her eyes with the hem of her skirt. "I'm fine. I'm running the company now, and I can't let a little freak-out sidewind me."

Dace started to correct her, opening her mouth to say, "Sideline," but the image of snake moving efficiently in an S shape up a dune of sand fit: ignore the reptilian.

They entered the low, one-story building and waited

while a young male receptionist in uniform informed the Commander they were here, then ushered them into his office.

Commander Cabassa stood and came around his desk to greet them. He wore his whites and authority well: he was trim though not tall, and without that instant advantage. However, the confidence he conveyed did not suffer from that lack. He stood erect, the tops of his shoulders rolled back though not rigid, and his torso rose up like a column powered by some force deep in his figurative root. His dark eyes held a lively light instead of the usual locked-down look of a military man. His head was shaved and his skin a burnished bronze like Dad's.

"Miz Banks," he said, turning slightly and nodding at Dace. He faced Rowena. "Mrs. Banks."

"Abad, it's been too long," Mom cried and threw her arms around him.

ACKNOWLEDGEMENTS

Hope Scoles, M.A., L.P., is a psychologist who appeared at the last minute at a course I was teaching on writing about encounters with the extraordinary. She blazed. Within a few short, in-class exchanges she provided the meaning I had sought to understand my own weird encounters and the meaning others attending had also sought. The insight and knowledge I took from her words struck and changed me, like the proverbial lightning bolt.

Tom is my husband who holds on and holds steady in the midst of whatever happens to be happening at the moment, a support I am very happy to have and enjoy. Thank you, Tom.

ABOUT THE AUTHOR

Karen Cavalli, née Lound, writes fiction and non-fiction. Her work has been published online and in books and has won awards including Outstanding Secondary Science Book. She is a graduate of Old Dominion University where she earned a B.A., and The University of Alabama's MFA in Creative Writing Program where she studied with Margaret Atwood. She has worked in technology for over 10 years. She taught a writing course on the topic of psychological descent at the University of Minnesota and in North Carolina. Her work in technology has taken her to India and China and allowed her to work with individuals in Mexico, the United Kingdom, Australia, New Zealand and the emirate of Dubai. She loves her local Savage library and volunteers there. She is married to Tom Cavalli. She can be contacted at kcgoodguide@gmail.com

CPSIA information can be obtained
at www.ICGtesting.com
Printed in the USA
BVHW082242041021
618107BV00001B/39